ALONE, HE FACED MAN'S GREATEST ADVENTURE . . .

"That was the first time I ever consciously thought of Robinson Crusoe in relation to myself. He and his island, me and Mars. Only I, born three hundred years later, could see it coming. Besides, I thought, strapping myself down and giving the rockets an experimental blast, those three centuries should have made a lot of difference. In Crusoe's day people did not know how skilled they were. They still imagined they would perish if left alone. Maybe I had got the same fixation. It was true that Mars had no breathable atmosphere, no drinkable water, and no sign of any source of food. So what?

"You might say that I had been born with a wrench in one hand and a blueprint in the other.

"I was going in to land."

And what happened then is a classic of science-fiction imagination!

CAST OF CHARACTERS

GORDON HOLDER

A human being, male, full grown, unmarried, in his middle twenties. Born in England, an engineer by profession. Worked on experimental rockets at the Australian proving grounds in 1957. Sole survivor of a crew of seven manning an experimental space-ship a dozen years ahead of its time.

MARS

A planet about half the size of Earth. Its year about twice as long as on Earth, its day about the same. Atmospheric pressure about that of a very high mountain top. Oxygen constituent not one hundredth. Temperatures ranging between those of Siberia and those of a London spring. Life presumed to consist of primitive lichens and bacteria. Arid. Windless. Thin ice in the polar caps that melted in the summer.

FIRST ON MARS

by

REX GORDON

Poor old Robinson Crusoe,
How ever could they do so?
They made him a coat
From an old nanny goat,
Poor old Robinson Crusoe.

—Anon.

isbn 978-1947964723

I

IT, THE LAUNCHING SITE around which we all lived in tin huts at Woomera, in the heart of the Australian desert, was not at all like a battlefield of World War One. It was true that there were craters, caused by the occasional misfire or explosion, but they were craters in dry earth, not mud. At dawn or sunset, you got an impression of gaunt and twisted girders dominating a landscape of flat blackened earth.

If you looked out over the desert to the westwards it was interesting to think that there was not a human being for a thousand miles. Only radar towers, every hundred miles, to measure the flight of rockets.

I used to get letters from my mother if from no one else. She asked me what we found to talk about, in a place that was as empty and desolate as I described. I said we had plenty to talk about and listed exhaust velocities, fuels, the metallurgy of firing chambers, trajectories, and displacements caused by turn-overs at high altitudes. There were plenty more items, but they were more technical and I did not think she would understand them.

I wasn't a fool. I hadn't been there six weeks before I realised that you either made your life around those things, along with the bearded university professors, the mathematicians in grimy shorts, the chemists with sun hats on their bald heads, and the physicists whose hair seemed to grow mostly on their chests, or you went out with the screamers. You could tell the screamer cases even before they began to paint their funny pictures or write away for correspondence courses on how to play the oboe. They would walk around with a shattered expression on their faces and, when you said something interesting about the new peroxide-nitric-acid comparison formula, they would back away as though they had seen something creeping up behind you. They never lasted. There was only one thing that kept men sane at Woomera, and that was rockets.

You may not think that men can feel strongly about rockets, about the difference, say, between one rocket and another. But we—at any rate all of us who had been out there six months or more—were constantly in a state of near-revolt. We were still tied to the ground control and allowed to do no more than shy one rocket after another along the range. It is surprising how sane men are when they feel deeply about something and are seething with discontent.

The Government didn't know it but just about half the rockets that were shied along that range had men inside them. The deaths, of which there were bound to be a few, were always put down to "lack of equipment due to inadequate finance". It was true, too. If we had had an R. A. F. Wing to assist us with the initial flying, and finance on the same scale the atom men were getting, we'd have been up to the moon before the Americans even sent up their artificial satellite.

In Woomera we seethed and fumed. We had two big rockets constructed, each capable of the seven-mile-per-second escape velocity from earth, and a little left for coming back, and we were held up for a year because no one could think of any reason to indent for the astronomical photographic equipment which would enable us to take the short-range pictures of the moon as we swung around it.

As for project M 76, which is what I am coming to, the only way anyone could think of protecting it from the prying eyes of visiting politicians, treasury officials, and our own more stupid Security guards was first to initiate a water project, sink an artesian well, build a water-tower, abandon the well because it produced no water, then hide the project in the tower. How would you have hidden a rocket standing two hundred feet high and with a diameter of fifty-six feet around the base?

It made us furious sometimes. All the best brains of sixteen universities going to waste because no one could think of a way of explaining why we needed three hundred-ton liquid oxygen tanks for rockets whose maximum all-up weight was supposed to be in the neighbourhood of thirty tons. I remember the bearded Professor Maxwell, his shorts held up by his tie and the sunburn peeling from his shoulders, as he held up his hands in supplication and cried to heaven: "Give me the bloody metal, and with these ten fingers I'll build the things!" He almost did, too. At least it was done by the heavy-gauge aluminium welding plant he first invented and then made. After that, we slit up thirty-gallon steel and aluminium tanks and rebuilt them as we wanted, lapped in layers like plywood.

As project M 76 grew inside its camouflage of the water-tower, I thought there would be murder done. It ended so that no mathematician was speaking to any other mathematician in the whole establishment. Every man had his own curve, all nicely calculated and involving the orbits of Mars or Venus, which he swore was the best within our limits of power and range. There were curves starting on one side of the sun, dipping in like a switchback then flying out in succession past Venus and the moon and so to Mars, returning to catch the Earth up after two hundred days. There were orbits that began as spirals, and orbits that were beautiful, so their opponents said, except that no space-ship, once it was in them, could ever break out again and come back.

There was only one M 76. By the nature of things that was all there could be. *After* M 76 had made a successful flight, and brought back the photographs of life, if not exactly towns on Mars, then, with world-wide interest aroused, would be the time to get official approval to build another.

The two seven-mile-per-second rockets had been held back. In those final days, when it was obvious that risks must be taken, the automatic photographic equipment had been indented for without any explanation of any sort. They would cover the moon at the same time as M 76 was sent to Mars—Mars because a motion-picture-camera picture could be obtained of its surface as 76 went into a tight orbit round it. Of Venus, such a picture would show only cloud.

"When I think," Maxwell said, standing inside the water-tower and looking up at the towering rocket that almost filled it. "When I think that if we could only have doctored the books to the tune of another three million pounds we could have made a landing, it almost makes me weep."

He was the winner of the mathematical stakes. It was his plan and his trajectory which had been the one chosen by our aptly-named Escape Committee, and he was to command the ship and navigate her and bring her back. The emphasis was on the bring her back.

I was interested in this. For six months I had been playing astronautical chairs. This was the game played by everyone who had any hope or interest in becoming part of 76's crew. You first jockeyed yourself into a position you thought was favourable and then proceeded to demonstrate how important your own speciality was to the smooth running of any rocket. I had done rather well. As Fuel Consumption Engineer, which I had then become, I had made one of our standard rockets, which we shot off down the range at intervals to keep things looking pleasant, turn a double somersault just over the Administration Building and land not quite a hundred yards away.

When they had picked the broken glass out of their ears and papers, I explained. Irregular firing. A slight slip by the automatics or one of my subordinates. Such accidents should not occur again. Except perhaps with M 76. I was worried about M 76. That the ship should carry a Fuel Consumption Engineer was most important. I might, if I was persuaded, go myself.

Such modesty had its reward. After an all-night sitting

the Escape Committee published its findings for the crew list.

My name was second on the list, right under Stephen Maxwell's. I went to the bar that night and really lived my shining hour.

A fortnight later seven of us climbed into the rocket and lay down on our couches and someone outside pulled the trigger.

2

SOME PEOPLE presumably do not know the sensation of being elevated in a rocket. They confuse it with being shot out of a cannon or taking off in a jet fighter or any of the other experiences that are apparently different only in degree. In fact a rocket flight is different in kind because it gets worse instead of better.

A rocket is a strange thing. It goes up nose first and comes down tail first. It moves in spasmodic fits and starts like an absent-minded grasshopper. For one thousandth of the time it betrays purpose and direction, but for the rest of the time it simply wanders, turning slowly end for end, or, unfortunately, spinning like a top. If you could imagine two ping-pong players, one in Europe and the other in the U.S.A., with the net erected in mid-Atlantic, then the rocket would be a leisurely-moving ball at some point between them.

After we climbed into the rocket we went to our rubber-lined couches and strapped ourselves down. I once saw a movie version of how people would travel in a space-ship. They climbed into something that looked singularly like the interior of an aircraft, sat down in comfortable seats, and went peacefully to sleep as the acceleration started. A real rocket is not like that at all. Considerations of space and equipment are identical with those in a submarine. Everyone knows how men live in a submarine, among a maze of pipes and machinery, tubes and levers. Their berths are tucked in or slung wherever an inch of space reveals itself amid instruments, wheel-valves, and highly explosive torpedo tubes. That was us, except that we had rather less space and rather more machinery. The only people who got any sort of daylight or any view at all were Maxwell and the maneuvering pilot, Petifer, who were up in a sealed compartment in the bow, and they made more use of periscopes, telescopes, calculating machines and chronometers than they did of the six-inch armoured windows.

The spin was the thing. That really upset us to begin with.

My berth was on the third level and tucked in between the air-purification plant and the softly-whining, oil-smelling gyros. A man called Bertram Hapton was with me there, lying slightly tensely looking up at our single yellow light-bulb. By 'slightly tensely', I mean he was supposed to be relaxed, but like me he found it difficult. There was such a racket going on before we started. We wondered if the team on the floor above were playing leapfrog or conducting a private war. In fact they were settling in, a little late, but no sooner had they quietened than hollow clangs began to take place in the packed spaces of the rocket down below. It sounded as though a giant machine were uncorking bottles, which it was.

Maxwell came over the loudspeaker. His voice echoed and reflected from the metal walls. "Prepare for take-off," he said. "Commander calling engine-room. Report on functioning of the automatics at second pre-take-off stage. Are they normal? Come in, Holder."

I looked at the row of dials in the panel above me. They had been carefully arranged where I could see them while bound hand and foot to my narrow couch. I spoke into the microphone that was rigidly suspended above my chin.

"What do you expect me to do about it if they're not?" I said.

"Five," he said.

"Four," he said. "Three, two, one."

I don't think any of us had expected the violence of the noise. I know my eyes widened. I could feel them. It wasn't the take-off that worried me. There was hardly, to begin with, any sensation of lift at all. It was just the vibration and screaming roar from every metal object in a world of metal objects.

The light went out. The filament had not stood the strain. It was a great beginning.

I noticed two things simultaneously. One was that we were evidently taking off in earnest. I could tell that because, as I lay there in the darkness, amid the screaming racket and the oil-smells, I could feel myself being forced down into my couch by a steadily increasing force. The other thing I noticed was a howl that permeated the screaming blackness. I could do something about that. I guessed what had happened. The noise level had built up until it had set all the speakers and microphones into mutual oscillation. I felt round carefully with the fingers of my left hand until I found the appropriate button, and cut them off.

Suddenly, like lightning through the darkness, a sensation of fear shot through me. My hand, where it had been on the switch, was settling down. My body seemed to be flattening out.

That is what I mean about a rocket flight getting worse and worse. Any normal conveyance, a jet fighter for example, accelerates normally, going faster by regular amounts in each succeeding second. Acceleration is a product of thrust over weight, and both are nearly constant.

In the darkness, apart from the unbearable din, which seemed about to shatter my brain-pan as it had the light, my mind was suddenly full of vivid figures. As a rocket flies, so its weight decreases. In no time at all, it is halved, then halved again. Visually, it starts off slowly, heavy laden with its weight of fuel. But it climbs with an accelerating acceleration toward the zenith.

I was being flattened by a geometrically *increasing* weight into my couch. I saw it all, the whole beautiful equation, before my mind gave up in fear and then blacked out.

I saw that equation in my dreams for years to come, and any experience of darkness and noise and the smell of oil would do it.

It is a good way to teach relativity, when you think of it. When a rocket burns away half its mass, it loses half its weight by the standards of those people standing looking up at it on Earth.

But for anyone in that rocket, assuming that the force exerted by the rocket motors is the same, the force of gravity—what they feel as gravity—had simply doubled. Sitting inside, you don't see that you're accelerating twice as fast.

I came to slowly with a sensation of my chest muscles rasping. My ribs seemed to recede about three feet above my body, then close in until they compressed my heart, and then fly out again. There was a panting noise that I hardly thought was me and a singing as of angels in my head.

Little bubbles of sound were rising to the surface and breaking all around me. The darkness was hollow, like a vacuum inside a bell. But as consciousness returned with a jerk, I opened my mouth to scream. I was falling, falling. . . .

Then I had no need to scream. Someone was doing it for me. Rather far away, but steadily, on and on, a human voice was screaming.

It took a violent wrench of mind, in that oily blackness, to realise that the rocket was not falling back to earth—I hoped it was not—but falling outwards (I hoped) at escape velocity, away from earth. It was with the same desperation as a parachutist pulls his rip-cord that I flicked on the switch for the communication system that connected me with the bridge.

Maxwell was there all right. As soon as he heard the speaker come alive above him, he yelled: "Stop that yelling!" Then five voices answered him at once, the speakers echoed against our metal shell, and the whole communications system went up in an oscillatory howl once more. It was a wonderful nightmare in the evil blackness.

That switch was the only thing I had to hang on to. I flicked it off and on again. It was heaven when I got a faintly hissing, ringing silence. The howler on the floor above had either been murdered or he had become even more frightened of pure noise itself.

Out of the loudspeaker above me came the strange sound of five men breathing as they seemed to fall through space.

"Captain Maxwell," I said. I regulated my voice and I kept my fingers right on the switch. "You may not be aware of it, but we can't see anything. We imagine we are falling and about to impact at any moment. Would you care to reassure us?"

"Reassure hell," he said.

It was not very comforting in view of our sensations.

Someone else said quickly: "Captain, are we falling back?"

I kept my finger on that switch. I thought the sound communications were going to go up in a howl again, but they didn't. Everyone else was afraid too, of what happened when everyone spoke at once.

"Not that I am aware of," Maxwell said.

"Captain," I said. "If you'd just tell us what you see."

"Rings," he said. "The whole universe is revolving round us. Rather fast. Too fast to see which way it's going."

After a while, he said: "Did you hear that, Holder?"

"Yes," I said, "I was only thinking. So in fact, neither you nor Petifer know where we are?"

"You fool!" he yelled at me. "How do you think I can take observations on stars and suns and moons and planets that appear as nothing but concentric bands of light?"

Then, as everyone tried to comment, the microphones

and speakers got out of hand once more. The howl built up, echoing in our space-ship in its vacuum as water-waves echo in a can in air. It rose in volume and up the sonic scale. It rose like a rocket to some ultimate zenith of pure sound, passed it and went out of view. That it was still ringing in a pitch too high for human ears was evidenced when the rest of the light-bulb gave way and showered our compartment with broken glass.

3

WE SORTED ourselves out in time. The falling sensation did not increase, but it is one of those things you never can get used to. We would have acclimatized more quickly to it, only, as the spin died down under the influence of the gyros the weightlessness was distinctly worse.

One man—no need to mention his name, he's dead, poor fellow—could not leave his bunk. He screamed when we tried to loose his straps. We could only leave him there and feed him, putting the food-syringes to his lips and pushing the plunger while he sucked. A pity. It cut him off from all the nicely sticky things that you are able to hold and eat and deal with in the weightless state.

Even before the spin quite stopped, Petifer was able to identify the small green band that appeared in the periscope astern as possibly the earth. Maxwell did a neat calculation on the internal and external diameters of the band and calculated our recession speed. From that and the area of furnace that was the sun he did a rough working of our position that put us somewhere on our course.

It was wonderful, everyone said, when the stars slowed down and you could see them wandering slowly past the window. They spent time up in the control-room, snapping scenes with cameras like tourists. It looked somewhat ludicrous to me, to see them making swimming motions with their bodies as they focused and tried to point their cameras. Maxwell had to stop it in the end and make an arbitrary rule that, however it might seem, what had been the floor was 'down'.

I spent a lot of time working on the gyros, which were running hot. They had not been intended for a solid three-day pull to stop a quite fantastic spin. I was not too happy when, to make a course adjustment, Maxwell gave the rocket motors a two-second blast. We came out of it in a spin again.

We had a solemn conference in the control-room after that, everyone with their feet on the floor and trying to look as though they were standing up. Subject: Holder's motors' left hand thread.

"It's the vertical take-off deflector-plate," I said. "It's either burned out irregularly down one side, or it's out of true."

They discussed various possibilities and eventually came back to where we started. It was the vertical take-off deflector-plate, step two, outside the rocket, about a hundred feet from where we were standing then.

We had an airlock and a self-contained diving suit, but no one was keen to mention them for a little while. We had tried it back on earth. With anything like one atmosphere inside the suit, in excess of the pressure outside, you blew up like a balloon and could not move an arm or leg or finger.

"The point is this," Maxwell said. "It's no use spinning when we're maneuvering near the planet Mars. In the first place the only pictures we'd get would be a lovely coloured blur. In the second it would be impossible to take the observations necessary to set our course for home."

We broke up that meeting. We had, after all, still nearly a hundred days to think about it.

In the privacy of our compartment, where the space-diving gear was kept, Bert Hapton and I made experiments with the suit. With four pounds of pressure inside it, in excess of the atmosphere we were using, you could move about with difficulty and even bend your arms, as though against giant springs, to do a little work. But would four pounds pressure, absolute, be enough to keep a man alive in space? I lay on my bunk and read the books. Between a third and a quarter of an atmosphere seemed quite reasonable. Men breathing oxygen had climbed Everest at that and flown aircraft higher.

I was to think of those experiments later. I was to think how, if I had not studied those books so intently, I might not have survived the accident nor lived the next five years.

Still, for the time being there I was, all set to be the hero of the expedition. Hapton looked doubtful when I asked if he wished to contest the honour with me.

I went to Maxwell. I told him I was ready to go out through the airlock and look at that deflector-plate. If it was a simple matter, I might even do a job on it.

I have wondered since if he had a presentiment. I remembered he looked distinctly worried. But I thought it was about me, and I felt fine.

"Don't worry about the pressure," I said. "We'll reduce it very slowly in the airlock. When it gets down to a third, I'll close up my suit. I'll remain plugged in with my telephone. If I find I'm immovable when we get down to zero in the lock, I'll tell you and you can fill it up again."

It sounded all right. He had to admit it did. For example, if I was in difficulty, or suffering from anoxia, I would not be able to open the outer airlock door, which was a complicated procedure in itself. If I could overcome that it was a fair bet that I could look after myself when I stepped out in space.

"I'd feel happier if we'd two suits," he said.

"Why?" I asked. "So that if I got into difficulties you could send another man out to get into difficulties too?"

He did not argue too much. He had not worked out how to take observations from or set courses in a spinning rocket—not with the precision required to find those tiny specks in space that were the planets. After all, he must have thought, if anything went wrong he would only lose one man, not the ship.

We set the time for the attempt the following day. In the meantime I got the suit up to the airlock and tried a couple of decompressions. It worked all right. The airlock was only a small steel shell on the skin of the ship, like the escape-hatch in a submarine, and intended to serve much the same kind of purpose. I could turn round in it, with the suit inflated, and face the outer door. That was enough to work on.

We began at ten a.m. by ship's time the following morning. I went into the lock and everyone stood around outside. When I closed the door, I could not see them, only the inside of the lock, which looked singularly like a metal coffin. I turned round early this time, to be ready, facing the other door, when the suit inflated.

It took a long time, a very long time. We took the decompression very slowly, pumping the air back into the ship so as not to waste it.

"Half an atmosphere," they said over the phone.

They did not need to tell me. I had a barometer with me and it was registering five hundred millibars.

At four hundred, I still felt fine, but I knew the insidious nature of anoxia. I closed my helmet and told them: "On oxygen now."

They could draw out quickly after that. Five minutes later, after a running commentary on their pressure needle, they told me: "You're in a standard commercial vacuum now."

"Beginning to open outer door now. O.K.?"

"Go ahead." It was Maxwell's voice. "Watch it. You've probably enough pressure still inside to throw it open."

To say 'watch it' was all right, but my suit wanted to force my arms out straight, like a scarecrow. It was only the walls of the lock that kept me in some sort of human shape. I fumbled and worked, and eventually heard a faint, faint hiss that was carried through my feet from the slightly open door.

"Opening," I said. With an effort, I gave it a push with my foot and suddenly looked out into space itself.

There were stars out there. Stars had always been in the sky before. So, as far as I was concerned, I was looking up.

I hung on to a handle by the door. It was as well I did. As soon as I let my body go and my arm straighten, I shot out and almost fell clear into space itself.

"What's happening?" Maxwell said. "What's happening? Give us a running commentary, do you hear?"

"Nothing," I said. "I'm outside, that's all." With an effort I managed to get my feet down to the ship. I stood up, with some sort of security on magnetic soles. The stars were still up, and the ship below me was down. She was floating in a sea which was the universe. It was rather pleasant. Close your eyes a little and you could almost imagine that there was a sea for the ship to float in and that the stars visible round the edge of her were reflections.

I turned round to face the sun, which was astern. That was bad. I could not see a thing. But I walked aft slowly, paying out the telephone as I went. Twice, pulling one foot, with its sticky magnets, from the deck, I almost pulled the other up too. I hung on to the telephone as to a lifeline.

I heard laughter over the phone. I felt annoyed. I said: "What the hell?"

"We can see you through the periscope," Maxwell said. "If you knew what you look like, tiptoeing down the rocket with your arms straight out on the end of a telephone."

"You look to your business," I said. "You see that no one pulls the automatic closing lever for the outer door until I come in."

I reached the tail of the rocket. I did not like the look of that. Theoretically it was possible for me simply to walk over the edge and stand on the new surface, but I could not rid myself of the feeling that 'down' was the way my feet were pointing. I went over cautiously.

When I stood up again it was clear that the rocket was standing on her nose, and it had been when I was on the sides that I had been in danger of falling off.

"You're out of sight," Maxwell said.

"I'm looking at the main deflector-plate," I said. "It looks as though someone hit it with a heavy hammer. I propose to take it off and either cast it adrift or bring it in. What happens if we're left without one?"

They had a consultation about that. I did not wait for them to finish. There was a spanner on my belt. By exerting my muscles to the full extent I managed to get my arm down to it. I set to work on the bolts of the plate standing at arm's length away from them.

"It doesn't matter about the deflector-plate of step two," Maxwell said. "By the time we come in for a landing we'll be working on step three."

"It's as well you said that," I said. "It's nearly off."

I unfastened the bolts. The thing just stood there. I hit it with my spanner. I felt the clang run up my arm but I could not hear it. The damaged deflector-plate began gently to sail away. I watched it as it started out on a wandering course among the stars, and then I turned round to go back.

It felt even worse, this time, to go over the edge from the tail of the rocket on to the sides. I could not escape the feeling that I would slide down the side and depart, with an increasing velocity, past the rocket's nose.

"What the hell are you doing?" Maxwell said. "You've come into view again. What are you crawling about like that for?"

"It's the constellation of Pisces," I said. "I was born in February. I like to keep it over my left shoulder all the time."

I got up on my feet again. I walked toward the airlock.

On arrival, I looked round sadly. But I could not think of an excuse to remain outside any longer, and I began the business of coming in.

I went down on my hands and knees. It was like lying down in a declivity or climbing into a grave. My arms were the worst part. I had to fold them in, then try to wedge them.

"For God's sake close that outer door again," I yelled. "It's the toughest thing yet, to stay in here."

"Sorry," Maxwell said. "Didn't know you were in."

The outer door began to close, eating its way across the heavens with its jet-black shadow.

I don't know what happened then. It must have been some mistake they made inside. The door closed all right. I am positive of that. And as soon as it closed its spring-loaded catches should have engaged so that no one could open it again without the complicated maneuver I had been through when going out.

So far as I was concerned, the strictures of my suit decreased as they put the pressure on. Instead of billowing out from me and making me a balloon man, it collapsed about me and then began actually to cling to my skin as the pressure outside exceeded that within. I did not attempt to open up my helmet, cramped as I was. I simply opened up my oxygen supply to compensate for the increased pressure outside.

I could hear then. I could hear them working on the inner door, to open up and get me securely inside and back on board.

I was shot out like a cork from a bottle. I must have screamed. I could see all the stars again, and the blazing sun, and the departing shadow that was the ship. My suit became all but completely rigid in an instant.

I was turning end over end in space and I could see the ship about a hundred yards from me, and still departing. It came into my line of sight and out again in successive moments. I had looped the telephone cord around me and it was that which was doing it, spinning me like a top.

For one dreadful instant I was left face towards the ship. I could see the telephone cord, my only lifeline, rigid and tight between myself and the terribly distant rocket's bulk. It was stretching like elastic and I waited for it to snap.

Instead, I began to swing in again. It was then that I found time to think.

I could see the airlock. Inner and outer doors were both wide open. The electric lights were burning in the interior and shining out into space.

I knew even before I hit the ship with the crash that stunned me and made my later movements slower. I knew that, on an instant, there had been no air left inside the ship at all.

I clung to the airlock door as I hit and my suit rebounded. There were wild, insane, and desperate instants as I fought with that intractable suit, which had too much pressure in it. I dragged myself inside, into the ship that had become a coffin. Scarecrow-like, my arms extended, crucified one might say, and mad with a sense of tragedy and terror, I struggled upright on the deck, flung myself forward, and closed the inner door.

It seemed an age before I even heard a sound, the sound of a shrill scream as the automatic air-plants of the ship pumped air into the quarters, refilling that shell, that emptiness, which for quite five minutes had been open to the cold, the outer vacuum of space itself.

4

WHEN THE pressure was normal enough to allow me some sort of free movement within my suit, I pulled the lever that automatically closed the outer door. Then I remained, holding that handle, stunned. And time went by.

I began to move. I had faced it then. I knew that I too must die. No one man could handle that rocket, turn her, take the observations, and bring her back to earth. But, although I knew I was to die, I had to find some purpose, some object which it was within my period to encompass.

I took off my suit. I looked nervously at the airlock doors. But they were closed and I knew they would remain closed. I could not conceive how the accident had happened. Some premature jubilation, some joking triumph, some omission of the tests. . . . But the floating bodies were the worst thing.

Two of them were left: Petifer and Hapton. Somehow they had not been shot out, like the rest of us, by the escaping air. But I could tell who they were only by the clothes. Nothing could have been guessed from those torn and staring pop-eyed faces. They were the terror of my new environment.

I began to work. Briefly, I laughed and was hysterical. All I had to do was to grab and touch and tow, but it was all I could do to put a hand out to them. When I touched them they moved. They floated towards me as though their icy hands would touch my cheek. I pushed them away and they rebounded and came floating back again after impact or started off on a course of their own, diagonally, towards the ceiling. I could not bear them. I shepherded them like sheep through an open store-room hatch, and slammed the door.

I slammed it so violently that I myself rebounded. I hung, arms and legs all ways, weeping and turning round and round in space.

I quietened. That whole level of the rocket still looked like a shambles. I went up to Compartment One, the control compartment, and closed the door behind me, shutting myself in as though to escape from an evil dream.

I lay on Maxwell's couch and looked out through the port of armoured glass at the dark universe towards which the rocket was still travelling. Blinding starlight in space of utter black. Away from the sun. I could not even see the planet Mars and did not know where to find it.

I lay there unmoving and wondered if it mattered.

It did matter. We had known we were taking a risk when we had built this rocket at Woomera. If she did not come back there would be no more rockets built for exploration and only inquiries and dismissals among the staff.

Cautiously, lying on Maxwell's couch, I felt the control buttons which had been under his fingers when he lay there even as certain engine controls had been under mine.

I heard the gyros whine in the engine-room as I pressed a button. There was no one in the engine-room now, but the machinery would work without attention for a little time. I continued to press the button. The rocket began to swing, as I knew because the heavens slipped past my window.

I closed my eyes as I neared a hundred and eighty degrees of turn. I felt the blinding power of unstopped sunlight on my face. Cautiously, feeling the sunlight depart again, I opened my eyes again.

I turned the bow of the rocket about the sun, turning the whole ship as I searched for the planet Earth. An inner planet from my point of view, she could not be at a great angle from the sun.

I found her after fifteen minutes' search: the pale green disc that was larger than anything but the sun itself with the pale white moon beside it, both in their second quarters.

My hand tightened on the control that would fire the rockets, blasting me home in this lonely ship to Earth again. With the planet before me, the temptation was almost irresistible. I could set my course exactly. I could fire all the rockets. I could plunge on and on.

My hand fell limply from the switch. Before I reached the position in which I saw the Earth, the planet would be a hundred thousand, a million miles away. If I were so foolish as to try to do the apparently simple, the obvious, my end would be a roasting death as I plunged down not on Earth but into the sun.

Maxwell could have told me the minutes, the seconds, the degrees of aim-off to apply, like the mathematical duck-shooter that he was. But Maxwell was dead.

Petifer was dead, the pilot who was skilled enough to make a landing on a planet when Maxwell found it.

They were all dead, even Hapton who had added to his duties those of cook and steward. Alone, I could not even get in touch with our base to tell them what had happened.

I pressed my button again, turning the rocket back to the bow-on position to her course, as shown to me by the gyro compass. That was the only certain thing I had to go on.

In time, this course, this orbit I was making, and that of Mars, would intersect. I wondered if Maxwell had left any instructions for making an orbit back to Earth from that position. I got up from his couch. I began a methodical search among his papers that was to last me several days.

I found papers with figures on them—papers and figures that were meaningless to me. And Maxwell had not brought any simple text-books on astronautics with him. There were none, for one thing. If there had been, he would have written them, would know them, and therefore would not need to bring them.

There was, of all things, a nautical almanac, which gave me the positions of the planets for every day and every hour as seen by a sailor or an airman back on Earth.

I wandered away through the ship in a daze. I found things to do. I scrubbed out the compartment that had been soiled with blood and torn-out lungs. I emptied the slops through the blow-out ejector mechanism from the ship. After one day, I began to drink. After two, I began to eat. Within a week I was taking my meals regularly and dividing my time into intervals of sleep.

But I could not work out for myself the whole theory of astronomy and the positions of the planets in relation to the sun and one another from such simple information as that the hour-angle was this and the declination of a star was that at a certain place on Earth on a certain day. Maxwell could and I could not. There was that difference between us from the start.

Perhaps, if I had been inside the ship, and working those airtight doors, instead of Maxwell, the accident would not have happened.

Each man to his trade. My present trade was to live, eat, and sleep, and wait for death and wonder in what form it would come. What disheartened me was the unbearable silence of the rocket, the stillness inside and the unchanging nature of the sky. I used to go down to the engine-room, to my old couch, and lie there, with the door closed, simply to listen to the untaxed gyros' softly melodious hum.

The dead men in the storage compartment had to be sealed in there. I could not bear the sight of that iron door and hung a sheet across it. The sight of the sheet was worse. I tore it down, and, on my constant passing between the engine-room and the bow of the ship, went through the central level with my head averted.

It was Shakespeare's idle fancy to speak of the music of the spheres. I could speak volumes about their silence.

When a ruddy disc detached itself from the otherwise unchanging constellations that lay in my path, I looked at it hopelessly and balefully from Maxwell's couch.

Mars. A planet about half the size of Earth. A year that was about twice as long as on Earth, a day that was about the same. Atmospheric pressure one hundred millibars. Oxygen constituent not one hundredth. Temperatures ranging between those of Siberia and those of a London spring. Life presumed to consist of primitive lichens and bacteria. Arid. Windless. Thin ice in the polar caps that melted in the summer.

I could see the polar caps. Now I knew where the planet

was, I could turn a telescope upon it. I had to do something, after all, and it was this that I had come so far to see.

I lost interest after a time. Everyone does. It's an experience when you first turn a pair of good binoculars on the moon, but you don't keep on doing it, even though its features are clearer and more startling than those of Mars.

It isn't as though you could see smoking towns and factories and seas and ships. Nor could I on Mars. It looked exactly, disappointingly, like what people like Maxwell had said it would be.

I watched it grow from a tiny, identifiable speck to a world the size of sixpence. When it grew to the size of a penny, and I could see two pinheads that were its moons, I began to feel nervous as I looked at it. I could do simple trigonometry all right. Enough to tell me of converging courses. I tried a few sailors' tricks I'd read about, like doubling the angle on the bow

That gives you your distance off as you pass the point or headland you can see approaching The answer I got was not quite zero, but it was very near it.

Maxwell had calculated too well. And he had talked of "Maneuvering when we get near the planet Mars."

I grew disgusted with that great thing there, that bright red penny that was growing on the rocket's bow. I suddenly hated the hours and weeks I would have to wait to die if, as seemed likely, I went into an orbit round it.

And then, grimly, I thought how it would be if I swung close past it and went off into space again, the sun growing smaller and the rocket getting colder as I swept out through the asteroids, past Jupiter and Uranus.

That was the first time I ever consciously thought of Robinson Crusoe in relation to myself. I thought of that incident after he was wrecked on the island. He is in despair about his prospects but he makes a raft of some sort to get out to the wreck. A current gets him and threatens to carry him out to sea. Instantly the island, which he had hated, becomes the object of all his thoughts and strivings. If he can get back there, he thinks, what an escape it will be from immediate death.

Me and Mars, just the same. Only I, born three hundred years later, could see it coming. The human race had had enough experience since then to give me foresight.

Besides, I thought, strapping myself down to the maneuvering couch and giving the rockets an experimental blast: besides, those three hundred years should have made a lot of difference. In Crusoe's day people did not know how skilled they were. They still imagined that they would perish if left alone and separated from their tribe. Maybe I had got the same fixation. It was true that Mars had no breathable atmosphere, no potable water, and no sign of any source of food. So what?

You might say that I had been born with a spanner in one hand and a blueprint in the other.

I was going in to land.

5

THERE WAS terror in my soul as I lay on my couch, in my straps, looking down on that red planet which seemed to swell until it ate up the heavens. What I was doing was suicide, but it was suicide on the grand scale. During all the previous history of our world men had risen from it, climbed and flown, but never failed to return. Never had they landed anywhere else. Who knew what effect it might have, this transfer of substance from one planet to another? Even if my dead body lay there, crushed in the wreck of the rocket on some plain of Mars, it would be Earth decay that would ensue, Earth bacteria that would be released.

Yet, grand as my project was, there was the grim human reality behind it all. To an Earth creature, born and trained to Earth reactions, it was terrifying to see that world expand.

Though still weightless and in free-fall, I had learned, in my time in the rocket, a sense of stability in weightlessness. It was now that I could see my fall visibly, appreciate the planet not as a speck, a disc which hung far from me in the sky, but as a sphere with a horizon which was growing hourly nearer, that I felt again in me that anguish of insidious fear. My nerves became taut as though there was in me some deep but atavistic urge to turn away, to climb into the tail of the rocket and hide my head. Repressed within me was an animal that did not understand and knew pure terror. Yet, below me, the world expanded and took form. No longer a brilliant disc, a blur of coloured light, it had substance, form.

I could see two snowy polar caps, one large, one small. I could see an edge of flatness to the disc where night lay across all the other side. I could see great bands and areas of vivid colour. This was a world, an actual world. I had seen photographs of Mars—who on Earth has not?—but those hazy miniatures, hardly impressing one with their detail nor even conveying the reality of their subject, were nothing to what I saw now. I could not, it is true, pick out, to any great extent, more detail. Certainly I could see neither cities nor evidences of life, nor even mountain ranges, evident for what they were, such as are visible in any photograph of the moon. This was a flat planet, without seas or great outstanding features, but it was its reality that was impressive, its overwhelming existence as a solid world.

I altered the angle of the bow of the rocket. It seemed to me that Mars was going to sweep past across my bow. It was in that way, momentarily left behind, that I would miss the surface and go into an orbit round it. I adjusted the rocket until it pointed away ahead along the line of Mars's apparent motion. Then I fired the rocket motors. I knew that it was probably my own death-warrant that I was sealing by my action. But, at the same time, my brain said insistently that I had a hope, a small hope but a true one. With the gyros, by the aid of which I could swing the rocket's bow which way I willed, I turned the ship until I could see again. Mars was perceptibly nearer, and it seemed to me that her relative motion was smaller now.

Hanging by my straps—I had the sensation of hanging now when my gaze was downwards, though I was dreadfully unaware of any weight and only of an increasing perception of a headlong fall—I wondered where on the planet, if I had the choice, I would aim to land. I could see the polar caps now clearly. The Southern pole was large, and the planet's surface near it was a dull dun brown. The Northern polar cap was small and, though from my height I could not see what caused it, I could see the vivid colour, red near the pole and green towards the tropics, that had been remarked so many times from Earth as being the characteristic of the Martian summers. Should I land there, where the season was evidently well advanced, or in the South where the spring had yet to come? Or in the tropics where the temperature, at least in daytime, would equal a temperate day on Earth, but where the water, or water-vapour as it had been supposed to be, would be more scarce?

In the event, I had no choice. When I was landing, I was too busy to know where I was. I was only accurate enough to keep away from the poles themselves.

With the gyros, I turned the rocket over. I shifted my gaze from the open port, which gave me a view ahead to the maneuvering periscope, which gave me a view below the rocket's tail. That was where Mars was now, and I was falling on to her. When with the magnification of the periscope, I saw the surface, dull and indeterminable as it was, rushing up to me, it was all I could do not to fire away my fuel at once. I knew I was falling now, and, sweating, I had to allow the fall to persist until I knew I was fairly in the planet's grip and would not skim past.

I do not know how many hours it took, from the moment I became fully engaged, until the landing. I know I lengthened the period of my agony and terror by firing the first blast off too soon.

Yet I dare not enter the atmosphere too fast. I knew that Mars had a very thin and tenuous atmosphere reaching up to great heights above the surface, unlike the Earth's which was thicker and more compressed. If I entered that atmosphere too fast, I would blaze and incandesce like any comet. I fired my braking charges, paused, and fired and fired again, desperately, glad of the giant weight which came upon me as I began to check my fall.

Then down and down again, more slowly now, but still too fast. I watched my periscope, then fired a charge again.

I came in through the upper atmosphere of the planet, at once terrified and exulting. Through the object glass of the periscope, I had a sudden vision of a plain.

Then rocks.

Not stable rocks but squares and boulders, fangs, that seemed to hurl themselves from a cataract of tumbling earth.

I knew fear then, wild and uncontrollable. Why had I thought to land on Mars? Below me was a wildly shifting, racing surface. Yet it was not the surface that moved, but I who was skimming past it. Though I came down lightly as a feather, the very spinning of the planet itself ensured that I would strike that surface at thousands of miles an hour.

It was then that I understood the madness of what I had attempted. I should have had Maxwell beside me, tracking an object on the surface with a swinging telescope. I should have had engineers, myself as it had been, watching the dials in the engine-room, informing me from moment to moment of the fuel used. From these observations the electronic predictor would have given me an angle at which to set the ship and the charge to fire.

My only hope was a rumbling sound, which began as a

whisper all around me, then grew into a roar. The atmosphere! It was at once my greatest danger and the only thing that could check my headlong tangential course around the planet. Was it burning the rocket's shell already? Was there a bright spark now, engendered by some roughness on the outer surface, which would spread like a chain reaction until I perished in a flaming track of light? I did not know. I thought of flame and death and tilted my ship and fired blast and blast again against the angle of spin of the world below me.

Yet I was falling now: an unskilled pilot, I could not counteract motion in two planes at once. I had a dreadful vision—so near, too near—of a rocky chain of hills, and then a line of red, and then an empty, endless plain. Hammering myself down into my couch, I fired my rocket motors with squandering wastefulness. My mind clung fantastically to a single hope: that Mars, so much smaller than the Earth, had only a third the gravity. Even though I was wasteful, clumsy, there must, there *must* be enough fuel and time to check my fall.

The first crash came then, a gigantic hammer blow. I had been ready for it a moment earlier, and yet, when it came, it seemed too soon. It was a shock like a gigantic kick along my spine. I felt myself black out, then live again. I seemed to turn over in space—rebounding?

The second crash came. I had thought to be flattened and smashed to pulp. I had a vision of the great rocket turning over like a falling wheel. Bow first or tail first this time? Nothing was more certain than that I could do nothing. My whole existence was buried and encompassed in a roar of sound as though my universe were breaking apart into its component atoms. And then the second crash, a blow that sent me in agony against my straps, blacked me out again, and resulted in a new, intolerable tearing roar. I had a vision then—whether through the port or the periscope glass I do not know—of a plain that was furrowed, amid clouds of dust, and wreckage spreading, rolling, twisted. The roar—it might have been my blood—rose to a climax.

As blackness intervened, I thought: "This is the end!" It seemed inevitable to me that my compartment in the bow, strengthened though it was, should be torn apart. Then, as the pressure rushed out of it, I too would be torn, my lungs exploded.

What a way to die, I thought. The Space way to die, the end of so many rocket ventures before they were successful.

6

SILENCE, oil-smells, darkness.

I was a submariner, a last survivor trapped amid the machinery of a ship on an unknown ocean bed.

I was an airman lying in terror after a crash. In another instant the explosion would ensue. Too late already. . . .

I seemed to be on my side and hanging from my straps. I could not see a thing. It was a hot, close darkness. Somewhere, striking terror to my very bones, an object fell with a tinny, tinkling sound.

I was on Mars. I remembered then. I was in a crashed ship. Around me was an unknown world. I was facing dangers innumerable. My consciousness seemed to come and go, and my spirits whirled. I had been successful! I had crashed, and was still alive!

But the ship could not still be airtight after the battering she had been through. Even now, not quickly, but inevitably, the air must be leaking from her. Soon I would choke and die. This was just an aftermath, a pause before the final terror.

I moved suddenly, struggling in my bonds. I had seen the faintest gleam of light from below me: the port-hole, apparently partly buried in the earth. That brought home to me the anguish of my position.

I tore at my straps, began to unfasten them, then clung to them. The moment I released myself I would surely fall. On to what? Was it possible that my eyes were becoming accustomed to the darkness as my world, my tiny world, took form around me?

Round? It seemed to me that the rocket was flattened and lying on its side. What was below me? Could I see if I turned my head? Wreckage. The litter from the entire compartment.

I struggled again, impelled again by fear of some catastrophe that must be imminent. Not till then did I remember that there could be no fire on Mars.

Slowly, standing, I came to myself. I had landed on Mars. Not well, Not badly. I was still alive in the remnants of my ship. The room was in a frightful state of wreckage. What was left of the rocket was evidently lying on its side. I was standing on the side of one of the couches at that moment.

Suddenly I moved as though impelled by all the fiends of hell. I scrambled, sliding and stumbling, to the port-hole. I put my face to it, and stared out greedily. But it looked downwards into torn earth. I went to the glass, the periscope that had served me in my landing. It gave out only a dark, dim light, and its glass was cracked. But I saw in it, as I adjusted the focus, a barren plain and a low horizon.

I sat down again on the bunk-side. So this was Mars. Outside was an unknown landscape with less air upon it than on the summit of Everest back on Earth. I did not know if I had arrived at dawn or sunset. It had been too much to expect to sight any sign of life. Perhaps there was no life. The changing colours of this planet, it had been suggested, were due to changing crystallisation of the rocks.

I was confined to the wreck. It was too much to think of it now as a vehicle, a rocket.

Why had I landed here? What had I hoped to gain, even

if I had been completely successful instead of only partly so?

Sitting in the dim, wrecked control compartment of the ship, I realised what it was. It was the sensation that even then gave me a feeling of irrational hope and power.

Weight. The stable, rational pull of the gravitational attraction of a solid body.

I pulled the cushioning from one of the couches. I laid it on a level surface, and laid myself on it. I thought.

I was on a not-completely-airless world at a distance from the sun that would have made the temperatures dangerous except for the windless transparency of the air. Certainly I would not dare to expose myself at night. I had, I hoped, air enough and food enough to last some time. I was then in what had been the highest level of the rocket. If the lower levels were intact, even the top two, then I would have a pressure suit and an airlock. But I must not be rash. The slightest mistake would be irretrievable.

Was I actually thinking of living on Mars? It seemed I was.

7

WHEN I HAD determined on my course of action, I got up. The first thing I did was to move about the compartment I was in. It took me most of the evening to salvage everything I could find in it. I realised that it was evening whenever the dim light began to fade. Quickly then, but deliberately, I made my first experiment. I went to the door, the hatchway, that led to the lower compartments of the rocket. If only, I thought, Maxwell had stayed up here, with that door closed, instead of clustering, with the rest of them, around the airlock. It was airtight, that hatch that had become a door, and it opened inwards.

If it would open, then there was air on the other side of it. If not, I was trapped.

I unfastened the catch and pulled. For a desperate instant I thought that it was hopeless. Then it came towards me and I slid down into the angle of the compartment. I quickly crawled up again. I was looking into a dark hole, for no lights were burning.

I climbed through. I thought I knew that ship. I had lived in her and I had known every inch. But move any room, however familiar, upon its side, and it ceases to be familiar at all. The very stairway that had led down no longer did so. It led across from one wall to another. Yet it was going to be no better in daylight, this part of it.

I felt my way along the ladder to the farther wall. There was another hatch there, that led into the engine-room. I felt for, and found, the handle that should have opened that. But, despite my efforts, it refused to open. Either it had warped and bent in the crash, or, more likely, there was a vacuum behind it. I crouched, clinging to the ladder, and thought.

I saw no reason to suppose that the electrical circuits of the ship were dead. The cells that fed them were in the engine-room, but it was not the engine-room that had made those clumps of wreckage on the plain, or this second bulkhead would have certainly received some damage. It had been the fuel tanks and the rocket motors that had been lost. The engine-room, with its gyros and electrical equipment must be still there. The lights had only gone out for the same reason that I had been left in darkness during take-off: the bulbs had failed.

After that first heavy failure of light bulbs a number of spares had been carefully wrapped and put in a cupboard in the galley. But where was the galley? It was in the level I was in and opposite to the airlock. But were either of those items up or down? I clung to the ladder-stairway and tried to visualise the relation between the way the steps had faced and the galley and airlock doors.

The galley was diagonally upwards. I had a frightful

scramble to reach it. By standing upright unsupported on the middle of the steps I could reach its doorway. That was the first time Mars helped me, with it lighter gravity. I could muscle myself up into it with little difficulty. To find the cupboard where the light bulbs were was another matter. The cupboards had been arranged to hold their contents irrespective of the angle of the ship, but even so I dislodged the contents of one shelf and was showered by articles which crashed their way downwards, seemingly a dozen times, before they lay still in the compartment far below me.

When I found the bulbs in the darkness, half of them were broken. Trying them in the galley light socket, I found one, exactly one, that sprang to light.

If Mars had had anything like the gravitational power of Earth that light would not have survived the crash, and nor would I. That was the thought that consoled me when I looked down in the dim illumination and saw the chaos that lay below me. The first thing I saw was the pressure suit, helmet buried and legs expanded, that looked like a body on its head among the wreckage.

Standing astride the galley doorway and looking down between my legs at the shadowed compartment, with its gleams of metal and areas of total darkness cast by my shadow, I thought that a sailor, wrecked in a submarine on an ocean bed, could hardly be in a position worse than mine.

Yet, looking, I wondered what it was, particularly, that worried me. I was making progress, wasn't I? I had a light now. I was doing fine.

Then I looked at that pressure suit again. Its legs, too human, stood upright from the wreckage.

Inflated, though they had not been.

Hurriedly, I lowered myself down from the galley. I took footing on the skeleton girder of the stairway, then lowered myself down again. I scrambled to that pressure suit with haste. It was inflated all right. Hard. But no one had been pumping air into it.

There was only one possible supposition. The air in the pressure suit was what had been there before. But the air in my compartments was leaking out. That they should have remained perfectly airtight after the crash had been unlikely.

In the semi-darkness, I stared at the closed hatch to the engine-room. It was through that the pressure-adjustment mechanisms lay. But there was an air-inlet, from the liquid-oxygen tanks, in each compartment. I scrambled across the room again. The pipe entered from what had been the ceiling. When I put my face against it, I could feel a steady draught. I was getting air, yet the pressure was falling. The pressure-adjustment was out of action. Either that or the oxygen tank itself was empty. I felt a crawling up my spine.

There was a wheel-valve on the pipe. I turned it off and waited. When I opened it again, there was a violent hiss for an instant, betraying the build-up of the pressure.

I crouched by that pipe for a long time. There was oxygen coming through it, but very slowly, not quickly enough to compensate for the fall in pressure due to innumerable tiny leaks in the rocket structure. The pressure inside my shell must be very little higher than that of the atmosphere of Mars outside. But richer in oxygen of course. Far richer. That was why I was living and moving normally.

I got up. I suddenly went out of that compartment altogether. I went back to the couch I had made for myself on the one level portion of the control compartment. I lay down there to think again.

I gave a silent prayer to God, or Fate, or Chance. A prayer of thankfulness.

Men had climbed Everest on Earth wearing open-circuit oxygen apparatus. They breathed the thin air outside but had it enriched with oxygen at a flow-rate of two to four litres every minute. On Everest and Mars alike, the pressure was high enough for that. Only at lower pressures still would the blood fail to absorb the oxygen that was there. I even knew the figures. A man needed 60 mb pressure of oxygen in his lungs. On Mars there was a pressure of 100, but only one per cent or less of that was oxygen. But an *enriched* Martian atmosphere could be breathed. Breathed normally, with the waste products being exhaled into the open air.

God, or Chance, or Fate, had showed me how. By a miracle, my ship, on crashing, had converted itself from the self-contained to the open-circuit principle. Or, to put it another way, given the crash, and the rupture of the skin of the ship, it had been bound to happen.

I had often thought that the will of God and the laws of Science were closely intertwined.

I lay there thinking how I could now go out on the planet Mars wearing not a clumsy pressure suit but only a cylinder, the weight of which I would hardly feel, and a simple mask. And my oxygen supply, which would only have lasted another hundred days or so, would now last longer. As for the air-purification cylinders, needed in all close-circuit systems to remove the carbon dioxide from the breath, I could do without them—unless Mars proved to have some actively poisonous constituent in her atmosphere. In that case I was quite finished.

I tried to sleep, but I woke up once, crying out in teror in the lonely darkness. Then the cold in my wrecked metal shell made me get up and move about.

8

I SPENT those dawn hours working on my mask. At all costs I must discover what lay outside. I took the oxygen cylinder from the useless pressure suit and made connections that recharged it from the ship's supply. Anxiously, I broke off work from time to time to look for the light of dawn on the patch of earth that was visible through the port.

The glass was steamed inside. When there was light, it looked as though there was a rime of frost upon the earth. I thought it as well that work on the airlock kept me busy until the sun was really up.

I had to simplify the mechanism of the airlock before I could get out at all. Working amid the wreckage, I thought that perhaps I should not go out. I should set everything to rights inside the ship and measure my resources. But, until I could get out and at least look at the world I had landed on, I felt like a trapped rat. I worked desperately, driven on by all the unanswered questions in my mind, but even so it took me longer than I thought.

I had set my watch at six o'clock during the dawn and pushed the regulator across to 'slow' to compensate for the day of twenty-four and a half hours instead of twenty-four. It was eleven by the watch by the time I was ready, in my mask, before the finished airlock.

I thought over everything, particularly my reasoning about the air. Now I could go, I stood there in the half-light, realising the chance that I was taking. Some planets, such as Jupiter and Uranus, had atmospheres of ammonia. No amount of enriching with oxygen would help a man if he once breathed that. Yet what choice had I? I had not crashed the ship on Mars merely to stay inside it.

I dropped quickly to my knees, to get into the airlock, which was at an angle downwards. I was driven forward as much by claustrophobia and fear of what I should find as by hope and expectation. I hardly thought at all, even with irony, of what an historic moment this was.

Yet it was an historic moment as I opened the inner door and climbed into the airlock. From the angle of the lock I judged that the outer door would just, but only just, clear the ground. After I had turned, with difficulty, and closed the inner door behind me, I had only to pull back a bar to be the first man ever to set foot on Mars.

I was in darkness. I had the bar beneath my hand. I hesitated a moment, and I pulled it. I did not set foot on Mars. I fell out upon it, in a hopeless scramble.

Blinding light. My eyes were unaccustomed to light after the semi-darkness of the ship.

Solid earth. A dusty, stony surface beneath my hands and knees. Perhaps I should call it not earth but 'mars'? I was rolling over and scrambling to my feet, or trying to, but finding myself under the curve of the ship.

My first, immediate reaction? Fear. Fear because I had taken a breath, instinctively as I felt myself falling. It did not smell like Earth air, nor taste like it. It was different enough to turn all my imagined fears into apparent facts. I sucked at my oxygen tube and waited for pain, for death. I thought of nothing but breathing, and yet it was moments before, on my hands and knees, I dared take another whiff. But it must largely have been composed of nitrogen and other inert gases.

I struggled up from my knees. I was not choking. As soon as I realised that, I had an impulse to move out from under the curve of the ship. As my eyes adjusted, I stared about me.

I was aware of wonder, savage interest, and acute despair.

The wonder came because my first overwhelming impression was of a level plain that was not a plain. To see the formation of the land on which I stood demanded a readjustment of impressions that had become a part of me. When, on Earth, the horizon is seen two miles away, it means that the land is not level but has a convex slope. On dead level ground, for a standing man, the horizon on Earth is five miles distance. This horizon was flat, and two miles away, and the ground was level.

The savage interest came because, after one sweeping glance around the horizon, I focused on the foreground and saw a flower. The implications of that were so big that I did not attempt to understand them immediately. I simply registered that before me, just beyond the torn earth caused by the crashing ship, was a patch of fibrous green with a tiny pink flower in the very centre, shaped like a diminutive anemone.

My mind said: Life! Then the disappointment set in, ranging rapidly downwards to acute despair. I had known what to expect, yet the sight of it hit me like a blow.

I had seen deserts. I had lived at Woomera, and I had flown out there by way of Iraq. I knew that deserts were not, for the most part, mere wastes of rolling sand. I knew that a man, if he had a flock of goats, could live on ten square miles of the average desert. But I did not see how I could live on this stony, dusty waste, with its tiny scattered flowers even if I had a whole planet of it to play with.

It was so bad, the emptiness and desolation, that I turned away from it, to look at the rocket I had left. But even there I saw not hope but only the miracle of my escape so far.

Not only was the tail of the wreck completely missing, but the rest was not only torn and scarred and twisted but strangely flattened. Only the part I had been in, say one-tenth of the whole and farthest from the impact, had been left to any degree at all intact.

I turned once more from the rocket again, and looked at the plain. There were the other flowers, I saw now, separated from each other by varying distances, but never by less than a yard at least. I took a few paces forward and went down on one knee to look closely at the first one.

It was all root-system, with infinitely soft and fine tendrils, green where they were above ground, running out in all directions. It was a delicate spider's web of a plant, with a lone flower in the centre. Certainly there was nothing like it on Earth, and it was very different from the primitive moss and lichens which had been supposed as the flora of

Mars. Far from being primitive, it was a highly developed form.

But a flower, I thought, still bending over it. Bees? I looked around the plain in all directions. I could see no sign of flying insects, and I could not imagine any. Bees were not exactly suited to high-altitude flight in rarefied air. The lack of oxygen would surely inhibit the growth of any truly active animal or insect life just as the lack of moisture made the plants rare and wide-rooted.

A thought came into my mind and was lost again. Bending as I was, I had seen a movement to my right. I looked more closely. I was wrong about the absence of mobile life. There was an insect. Six inches long, and apparently all legs, it had a spidery shape, with a small but fleshy body. I wondered that I had not seen it before, for the body, what there was of it, was a brilliant red. And then I saw the slowness of its movements.

It was bending over a flower, into which it had inserted a long proboscis. It sipped like a bee. But it moved, even when it left that flower and moved toward the next, like an Earth animal in slow motion. I was fascinated by that terrible slowness. Only a creature whose metabolism was very, very slow could move like that. And only a creature without enemies could survive if it did. I was looking at life on Mars—perhaps the only life on Mars.

I stood up. What had I been thinking when I saw the insect? Something . . . something about the plant. I could not remember.

I walked a little away from the rocket, turned round and looked at the horizon. I walked round the rocket and looked again. To the west were low, dune-like hills. Apart from that, in every direction, there was the plain. And the horizon lay closely round me. In no direction could I see more than the land I could cross in less than an hour on foot.

What should I do? Examine the rocket or set out across the plain? I stood for a minute in indecision, noticing that my breathing was deep but steady through my mask. I saw another insect, moving with the same, painful, incredible slowness of the first one. That was all there was in my range of vision: the flowers that must grow from the nightly dew on the scattered earth, and the insects which supped from them. I must see if there were anything more to see.

Desperately, I set off to the westward. Walking in that light gravitational pull, I felt strangely hampered by the movements of my own legs, as though they should have been longer so that I could take easy, flying strides. Those insects, I thought. The amount of energy they used must be incredibly small. But then, the rate at which they could burn their food, their fuel, in this thin and barren air, must be even smaller, slower. Suppose I gave one of them a whiff of oxygen. Would he leap like a flea on Earth, or would he simply shrivel up and die? Again, I tried to recover the thought I had had about this plant, but I could not do it. Something, surely, about the nature of life on Mars.

I approached the low hills with surprising speed. There were only the same plants, the same species, all the way. There was a certain order about their deployment on the ground. On level ground, or on gentle slopes to the north or south, they were placed regularly, each one four feet from the next. On slopes to the east, they had a wider spacing. In hollows, and on west-facing slopes, they were distinctly thicker. I was thinking of this when I saw one of the insects' nests.

Naturally they would have nests, I thought. Like bees on Earth. They would forage during the daylight and retire at night. On Earth, flowers could only be reached in quick succession by creatures which flew. Here, nothing grew tall. The flowers were hardly more than half an inch from the ground, and the insects stood easily over them. It was as though the bees' function, on Earth, had been taken over by the ants, the latter, with no birds in the sky, having prospered and grown big.

The nest was a mound, three feet tall, with an opening at the top. An insect was climbing slowly and painfully up, another was climbing down. I shuddered. I thought that such nests might be a source of honey. I imagined myself eating it. . . .

I looked back at the wreck. I would have to be careful. It was nearly out of sight. But the low hill was before me, of rounded sand-worn rock, and completely barren. It was hardly a hill at all, being more a diminutive rocky outcrop from the dust.

I warned myself as I climbed it. I felt my breath coming quickly and I detected a strange weakness in my limbs and lack of purpose in my mind. Even breathing oxygen as I was with every breath, I would have to go easy on this planet. The pressure was very low. If I wished to survive, I would have to match the Martian slowness.

From the top, I saw the plain extend into infinity all about me. In the distance, which might be ten miles away from my eminence, the land looked faintly pink with the tiny flowers. No change. No new thing any way I looked. Only in a kind of gentle hollow, which I judged to be two miles distant, did the vegetation seem a little thicker. But I saw no reason to suppose that even there I would find new species of plants or creatures.

I walked back to the rocket. As I went, I suddenly thought of what had occurred to me about these plants. It was the fibre roots, their distribution on the ground. Lack of water was their limiting factor. Lack of water had more effect on Earth, there were more things growing. And on Earth, plants like these, in any desert, would be completely eaten by lizards, active and voracious insects, cattle, goats, and sheep. And the reason why those things did not exist on Mars was the lack of plants to increase the oxygen content of the atmosphere.

I doubted if there would be any more active creatures than the insects I had seen. If there were, they would eat the plants, denude the planet, and then there would be no oxygen at all. I was thinking now, numbly. . . .

It was strange, I thought, how I had had to leave the Earth altogether before I realised that it was only the preponderance of water on our planet that made the plant life preponderate over the animal, thus supporting animals at all. Even on Earth, where there was not enough water the plants were soon eliminated by the warm-blooded creatures that ate every living thing, then died themselves.

Water was the key to life on Mars. The pressure was sufficient, the actual pressure of the inert air. But water—! Despite my own self-warning I hurried back to the rocket.

I went round the tail. I turned and looked back along the furrow that the machine had torn in the desert when it landed. There was nothing but tangled, scattered wreckage there. But inside?

I entered the shattered hull by a gaping hole. There was a fuel tank, still intact, one out of the many we had started with. I scrambled in, in semi-darkness, over sharp edges of twisted metal. I saw the liquid oxygen tank, which I knew must be there. But water? We had used it, and not only for domestic purposes in the galley. It had been an essential constituent of our fuel mixture, limiting the temperature of the firing chambers. There ought to be a thousand-gallon tank. There must be a thousand-gallon tank.

There was fear in my heart as I scrambled through the wreckage, the twisted girders, the broken machines. I had to crawl on my hands and knees, lever myself up through gaps, and peer through the dark shadows. Like any diver in any wreck, I was afraid of being trapped there. But my fear that my oxygen might give out while I was deeply involved in that portion of the wreck was conquered by my feeling that there must be water. Fleetingly, strangely, I felt a kind of faith. It was as though I were fated, and there must be everything I needed.

Then, dimly, not above me, as I had expected, but below me, I saw the tank. I stopped and stared in horror.

Even from where I was, I could see that it was split. It was in that portion of the rocket which, against the ground, had borne the brunt of the final crash. I crawled down to it and was not content until I had taken the cover off and put my head inside.

There was enough light penetrating through the crack to show me that there was nothing at the bottom but a shallow puddle.

I do not know how long I remained there, while the meaning slowly came home to me. I was as though stunned. After the accident, the arrival at Mars, the landing, and finally my discovery of a way of breathing and moving about on Mars, it seemed somehow impossible that I should find myself without the one thing which I had decided was most necessary to life on this arid planet.

It was as though I had had a vision of myself in my mind, of how I would live, ultimately, with plants growing under glass and supplying food and oxygen and all the things a man needs to live. It was true I had realised there would be difficulties. Because there was no fire on Mars, I would have great difficulties to solve when I began any sort of manufacture. But it had been there, my conception of myself as a skilled, ingenious man, who would and could survive.

But now no water. None but the little, twenty gallons maybe, that happened to be in the service tank in the living quarters of the ship

I withdrew my head from the tank and sat down beside it, inside the wreck, still dazed.

I went over my reasoning again. I had seen the plants that were the vegetation of this part of Mars. They had a widespreading surface root system which appeared to indicate that they grew on the nightly dew which settled on the earth. On the west-facing slopes, which would get the sunlight latest in the morning, they were thicker, as though they grew better where the moisture lasted longer. Where the ground dipped to a hollow, they grew, comparatively, in profusion. But where the ground was arid they hardly grew at all.

I looked down between my feet to the crack in the rocket's hull where the water had run out, and almost gave a cry. The plants were growing there, white and bereft of sunlight, but in profusion, like some sickly, white jungle.

But the water was gone, wasted, and absorbed into the sponge-like earth. The plants could not be grown again, with glass over them, though that thousand gallons would have lasted many, many days.

Because I had no water, I could not make a garden of thickly-growing plants. Because I had no garden, I would soon run out of both food and air.

For a moment, I almost went mad. It was the strangeness of my reasoning, the unaccustomed channels along which it had to flow, the chill in the shadowed interior of the rocket, and the silence, the deathless silence of that frightful, desolate, and lonely planet. I feared, too, that the oxygen in my cylinder would soon give out.

I scrambled madly out of that wrecked portion of the ship again. I went back to the airlock, and let myself in, with difficulty, into those tilted compartments which offered, at best, a temporary haven until the steadily leaking oxygen gave out there, too.

9

IT IS STRANGE what happens to a man when he faces death.

I tried not to think while I made myself a meal in that hopeless, upturned galley. It was afterwards that I had to face it, when I lay on my improvised couch amid the internal wreckage of the shattered rocket. The glow of the single naked light bulb seemed to hypnotise me as it reflected dully from the metallic surfaces around.

I had seen enough, during my trip outside, to know now what I had. I had air and food and drinking water for perhaps a hundred and fifty days. After that, nothing.

Nothing? I had the wrecked machinery of the rocket. I had a great tank of fuel which on Earth would provide me with power enough to drive me around the globe in search of irrigation water if I had to go to the polar ice-cap in search of it. On Mars, due to lack of oxygen in the atmosphere, that fuel would not even burn.

I had one electric battery, which fed my one good light. The battery would not last a hundred and fifty days. The bulb was burning dimly already. In space, we had used a little internal combustion engine to charge it, feeding the engine with fuel and oxygen and allowing the exhaust to discharge into space itself. Now, I could only do that if I were willing to use up my oxygen at an appalling rate with no hope of replenishment when it was done.

What else had I? There had been no spare stores or pioneering equipment on the rocket. There were two useless gyros and a host of pumps, some broken, some sound, and many miles of piping. The pumps had been used for feeding fuels and liquids to the various motors. Most of them had been electrically driven.

I was on a planet with an atmosphere so thin that the sunlight, though weaker than on Earth, yet seemed far hotter when it shone. Yet in the shade the temperature was hardly ever above freezing. At night outside, it must be very cold. And that thinness of the atmosphere was what really affected the supply of water. If I were to go out and dig in that hollow I had seen, in search of water, and if I were miraculously fortunate enough to be able to make a well, the evaporation from the surface of the water I exposed would be so rapid that the well would soon be dry again.

Probably if I went even to the polar regions—though I could not, being tied to the main oxygen tank of the rocket —I would discover that the snow there did not melt in sunlight. As had been observed of the snows of Everest, it would never pass through the melting stage but evaporate straight from snow to vapour as soon as the temperature rose above a certain figure.

Only at night—I looked at my watch and saw that it must be coming night again outside the rocket now—would a light dew settle and turn at once into frost, falling from the air that was too thin to support the burden of its vapour. And only the plants with their fine nets of radiating roots could seize that dew when it happened to melt too slowly in the morning.

I turned and twisted on my couch. I tried to relax and sleep, but I could not. There was one other feature of my environment. What was it? The insects. Because they moved so slowly, they managed to sustain themselves directly from the plants. Perhaps, for all I knew, they drew not only moisture but oxygen from them too, in another form. I was not in a position to investigate the chemistry of life on Mars.

Or was I? Certainly I could not sleep. Yet I could not go out again, from the rocket. My life on Mars, short as it might be, seemed fated to be divided up between some eight hours of work in daylight and sixteen hours of each day hiding inside my shelter.

But, try as I might to be positive in my thinking, to take lenses from the broken telescopes and make myself a glass with which to examine the microscopic, bacterial life of Mars, my mind kept coming back to the thing I lacked, which I needed.

If only I had a fire. If only fire were merely possible in the Martian air. What was man without a fire? Could he ever have advanced from the cave-man stage if it had not been for the lucky accident that, on Earth, most organic substances burned, if they were merely ignited by flint or friction, in the atmosphere of that beneficent planet? What civilisation would ever have been possible, even on Earth, if there had been no fire?

For a while, on my couch in the wrecked rocket, I lay quite still. I remember that I was just beginning to shiver as the temperature fell with the falling night. For an instant my problems passed beyond the bounds of personal fear and horror. I saw them on a greater scale, against the background of the nature of Man himself.

What was Man—what was I—but a creature who had, by a series of lucky accidents, learned to live in trees and so developed hands, learned to come out of trees and so to walk erect, learned to use tools to guard himself, because of the hands he had, and so developed brain? And what would all those accidents have done for him had it not been for the greater one of his discovery of fire?

The lack of fire suddenly seemed to me to be overwhelming, greater even than the lack of air or water. With fire, Man had learned to make machines. With fire even I might have made things for myself, made vehicles, sunk wells, and used the power of fire in a million ways.

Man without fire was a naked, helpless thing, hardly better than the tree-rat he had once been a thousand million years ago. Even three hundred million years ago Man had had fire, and tools and implements of flint. . . .

I slept at that point. I cannot quite explain it. It must have been a combination of nervous and physical exhaustion. Yet at one moment my mind had been nervously active, overtired and sleepless, and the next it was dead.

I dreamed most horribly during that second night on Mars. I dreamed that I saw myself, a latter-day Crusoe, on some fantastic bicycle I had made from bits and pieces of machinery. Instead of a goatskin coat, a parasol, a gun over my shoulder, and a parrot on my arm. I wore an oxygen mask and carried a microscope and a collecting box for specimens. My bicycle broke down when I was too far from the rocket to walk back before my oxygen gave out.

I dreamed again. I had built a perfect dome of glass in which plants flourished. I moved among them, tending them, like a gardener in a hot-house. I watered them with a watering-can, and breathed in the sweet-scented air which they exhaled, exchanging the carbon dioxide in my breath for the oxygen in theirs, and eating them too, plucking perfect fruits from them. But they were attacked by some wilt, some blight, some rust that I could not identify. I watched it spread up their stems and leaves and saw them die. Then I saw that the rust, a fungus or a virus as it might be, was growing on my hands. . . .

I awoke, shivering with horror, in the middle of the night. It was the cold that had caused my dreams, I believed. I sought around for garments and coverings and lay down to sleep again.

I could not. I was a man, and Man was a helpless creature who only by a chapter of accidents, by climbing trees and coming down again, by discovering fire and using tools, had acquired a brain. He was nature's joke, who lived purposelessly, brutishly, and knew he was going to die. I lay there in darkness now, and saw life bleakly.

Slowly, I grew warm in my extra coverings, and as I did so, my thoughts began to change.

Suppose, I thought, Man had not climbed trees. Suppose he had not discovered fire, would there never have been anything at all like Man on Earth? Would no living thing ever have become conscious of itself, as I was, nor of the universe around it? Would the stars and the planets have wheeled in their courses for ever, unrealised and unknown. with no eye cast up in wonder? Perhaps it was because I knew I was going to die that I thought about such things.

Yet I seemed to contemplate a mystery. Man was the only

self-conscious creature. He was the only living thing to inquire into his place in the universe, to have gods and thoughts beyond his lifetime. Without Man, it would be true to say that the universe itself would have no consciousness of itself. Then, indeed, it would be blind and purposeless.

Strange thoughts, it might be thought, for a perishing castaway in a wreck on an alien planet. But they were not without significance to myself.

It was surely the warmth, the extra garments that had done it. Nothing else could explain the flood of comfort that seemed to settle on both my body and my mind. What did it matter, what could it matter, that I had decided that if Man had not come into being in one way—by climbing trees, by inventing fire—then he would have done so in another? What did it matter to me that I had conceived of Nature suddenly as active in life with a force that went round or through or over obstacles? That I saw life, on this and every other planet, as unstoppable, a part of a process into which it was beyond me to inquire?

I was still lying outstretched in the wreck, with only a hundred and fifty days of life before me, confined and brutish, without hope, and ending, surely, in stark madness. Yet I slept, then, with the sweet innocence of a child, dreamlessly, and in comfort.

10

IT WAS DAWN when I awoke. A grey light was penetrating through the half-buried port-hole. I sat up and rubbed my aching cheeks. Despite the ache, my face cracked into a grin again. I climbed through to the galley, drew a quantity of water, and did what I had not dared to do before. I switched on the electric stove. It did not matter. I would soon have power to charge the batteries.

I thought about it as I sat eating breakfast on the horizontal bulkhead of the galley. It was a shame to cheat on the difficulties that would have faced my imaginary prehistoric man if he had lacked a fire. But he would, presumably, be mobile. He would not have had to content himself with what could be found in a two-mile radius in a desert. He would have found, in the end, those raw chemicals which, mixed together, produced heat. It might have taken him another hundred thousand years before he discovered and was able to make an artificial fire, whether there was oxygen in the air or no. But I had not a hundred thousand years to waste. I had to deal with the circumstances that I had, and do it quickly. The scientific approach was the thing. I pushed my breakfast aside and went back to the control-room.

The instruments immediately available were a barometer, a thermometer, and half a dozen gauges of various types. I did not reject anything. I unscrewed the lot and took them to the airlock. I had to take an oxygen pressure gauge back again while I charged my cylinder, but I was not worried. It seemed to me that there was stuff enough in the wreck for me to live on. Instrument-making would not become a hobby of mine for a year or two.

I adjusted my cylinder and my mask, and went out through the airlock, taking my equipment with me, including my gauges, a screwdriver, and an adjustable spanner. Those were my tin-openers, to open up the planet Mars.

I was earlier than the previous day. By eleven a.m. I knew from the previous day, the atmosphere would be comfortable. By afternoon, it would be distinctly warm. At present it was cold, particularly out of the sun. A man does not want more than a hint like that. I used the thermometer immediately. The instrument registered ten degrees of frost in the shade and seventy degrees Fahrenheit when exposed to the rays of the small, hot, rising sun. The thin atmosphere of Mars was responsible for that. On Earth the direct heat of the sun would have been masked and the shadows warmed by the thicker air.

Temperature difference eighty degrees. Atmospheric pressure one hundred millibars. I scratched my chin where the mask was chafing it. I would have to do something about that mask.

I wondered if the fuel would do. God knew, I had enough of it, and it was useless as fuel so long as I had no atmospheric oxygen to burn it in. A synthetic petroleum mixture, we had mixed it with oxygen when firing it in the rocket motors. Now I thought of it in another fashion. I laid my instruments carefully on the ground and took my spanners with me into the engine-room, through the hole in the gaping hull.

I unfastened the drain cock on the fuel tank cautiously I thought maybe I might be in trouble. Many liquids boil at such low pressures, and I did not want to be scalded by a freezing jet of alcohol steam.

It was all right. In the deep cold of the shade of the rocket's interior, I merely ran off a little liquid which rapidly evaporated, surrounding me with heady, heavy fumes which I could smell through my mask as I drew in outer air mixed with oxygen. On Earth, I would have been afraid of fire. On Mars, I merely shut the tap again and thought.

I looked around the engine-room. The one thing I had was a superfluity of pipes and pumps. There was a six-inch fuel pump connected to that very tank, which had been used to deliver the mixture to the firing chambers. There was an oxygen pump, which, if used for its intended purpose, would deplete my supply of air in almost no time at all. There was a one-inch water pump connected to the domestic supply line, and a larger pump which had taken water to the motors, both connected to the cracked and empty tank There were pumps connected to the hydraulic machinery. The only thing I had more of than pumps was electric motors, and all were useless unless I intended to waste my substance on them.

Useless, that was, connected as they were.

I set to work. The first thing to do was to find two positions, one which would be in sunlight all the day and the other which would be in shade. When I had found these, I began to disconnect lengths of piping. It was slow, tedious work, disconnecting joints and elbows and remaking them. I had to make a grid of parallel pipes in the sunlight and another grid in the shade. Not all the joints and sections were intended for my purpose, and I had to improvise. But it was reassuring to discover, at the end of the morning, that in the hot pipes in the sun my petroleum vaporised at once, and that in the cold pipes in the shade it condensed again and became a liquid.

I worked on through the afternoon. I could see that the result was going to be very crude. I used a one-inch pump to pump the fuel liquid into the heating pipes. A six-inch pump was all I could find, the largest that is to say, for the boiling petroleum to drive. I hoped my memories of water-tube boilers on Earth was adequate. I stood back and looked at my work from time to time.

It happened even before I finished. I had run a quantity of fuel into the cold pipes, which were used as the condenser, and turned the small pump by hand to force some of the liquid into the hot pipes. The big pump, driven not by steam but by boiling petroleum, made one stroke, then another. Before I knew what was happening, she was running merrily away. I had to wait until the charge was exhausted before I could connect the two pumps.

The sun was sinking. I had not expected my heat engine to work at that time of day, though I had gone to the extent of burying the cold pipes in frosty earth which had had no sunlight on it. I had thought: perhaps in the mornings only, when the temperature difference was greatest. But I had forgotten that though the pressures I was dealing with were very small, so was gravity, and therefore friction, on Mars.

I stood back and watched the wheels go round. I doubt if anyone ever had the same sense of creation as I had then. I drew no power from the machine. I simply watched it. I had done that. Petroleum was being pumped into the hot pipes where it boiled in the sun's heat. The vapour developed pressure enough to drive the big pump. The big pump drove the small one. The vapour, after passing through the big pump, went through the condenser and returned as liquid to be pumped again by the small pump. The same petroleum went round and round, again and again, like the water in a marine steam engine. It was not burned or used at all, except for losses due to leaks. The power source was the sunlight and a temperature difference of only sixty degrees Fahrenheit.

Heat engines were more efficient on Mars than on Earth just because the atmosphere was so thin: because the heat which came from the sunlight was not distributed equally over the surface of the planet by that vast reservoir of heat which was the treacly atmosphere of Earth.

Begrimed, my hand trembling as it held the spanner, I watched those two pumps working, the one driving the other. I was the happiest man in the entire universe at that moment. Wheels were going round. I had a source of motive power. Already, even with my machine in its first, crude state, the electric motors, which I had left connected to the pumps, were acting as generators and showing a voltage on my meter.

Power.

Power in a form more flexible and more usable than fire. Beautiful power. With that, it seemed to me, I could do anything.

The sun slowly sank, and, as the shadows became long across the empty plain, each little hollow and curve of land becoming a pool of darkness, the machine came to rest, running more slowly and finally stopping. But I did not care. It had run and, when I went into the closed compartment of the rocket again that night, I felt confident enough to use my light freely, and to use the battery power to cook myself a meal. Late that night, I found myself sitting on my couch, with a blanket around me it was true, but sitting up, and looking with a kind of wonder at my own hand, my right hand, in which, quite causelessly, I held a spanner.

11

I MUST have stayed up late that night. There was, after all, no one to please but myself. I overslept the following morning. When I awoke, it was to the tune of two pumps hammering away wildly outside my compartments in the rocket. It might have been thought that, for a moment on waking, I would have imagined myself back on Earth, where machinery sounds were common. But I did not. I came to full consciousness on an instant, and knew what the sound was. I leapt and staggered from my couch, put on my mask and harness, and went out into the cool morning. I connected the electric motors on the pumps in series, and tore out wiring from the damaged portion of the rocket to connect them to the battery. I stood in the early sunlight and looked at an ammeter which indicated a steady charge. Then I went back inside for breakfast.

It was a crude method of adjusting the voltage of two motors so that they charged the battery which had once driven them. But it worked for days, until I found time to make my machine more efficient. Then, my power needs having risen, I adjusted the brushes of the motors, took two cells out of the battery, and was able to draw off a good and heavy charge.

But such niceties were for the future. On that, my first power-driven morning, I was still too much aware that, though I had a source of heat and energy, I was a long way from converting electricity into water and air.

Always, until I had my engine going, I had thought of the solution of my problems in biological terms. I had thought that the only possibility of my survival lay in getting together a sufficient quantity of plants under air-tight glass. Perhaps, in the long-term view, it did. But glass was something I was short of. All I had were still more pumps and electric motors, piping, burst tanks and sound ones, steel plates, and two beautiful but completely useless gyros.

With this material, I needed a simple and direct solution of my immediate problems.

Water was easy. I solved that problem in six hours flat. I had observed that at night, when the temperature dropped over the desert plain, the dew settled down and turned to frost. It was on this frost, when it melted in the morning, that the surface-rooted plants were living. What I wanted, obviously, was large quantities of dew. To get it, I needed to duplicate the conditions of a sudden drop of atmospheric pressure.

The burst water tank was the obvious choice. What took me most of my time was the job of repairing it. On the face of it, it was a simple welding job, with leads taken from the battery, but whoever had installed that tank in the rocket had not contemplated it being cracked and then re-welded while *in situ*. I had to do some sawing first, before I could get at the broken parts.

I used the old oxygen pump to draw out the air. The only difficulty at that stage was to get the right adjustment. The air had to be sucked out of the tank, when it was gas-tight once more, and, as a continuous process, fresh Martian atmosphere had to be allowed to whistle in slowly, undergoing a drop of pressure, and therefore of temperature, as it did so. The theory was that the dew, formed as in a cloud-chamber, would condense on the walls of the tank and run down. But it is difficult to do this kind of thing when the total outside pressure is only a hundred millibars. First the oxygen pump, which had a far too powerful motor, tended to run away with me, and also to use too much power. Then, when I had fixed that by dismantling the thing and working on trial and error with the field coils, the jet to allow the air into the tank proved to be a matter of critical dimensions. I had to drill an assortment of plugs in the end, and try them one by one until, at the end of a quarter of an hour's pumping, I got a trace of water in the tank.

As I say, it took me six hours' steady work, which I later thought, when the thing was working, and water was accumulating visibly every time I opened up the manhole, was rather good. At the time, I remember, it seemed awkward and an unnecessarily laborious business.

The truth was that my mind was not wholly on the job. I was worrying about the far more difficult problem of getting oxygen. The only immediate source of it was the Martian air, and the best Earth estimates were that there was only one per cent of it in that. I was getting down on equipment, too. I had only a few small pumps left, largely from the hydraulic system. The gyro motors were intact, but by no strength of imagination could I see any way of making a gyro motor produce air.

It had to be the pumps. I could only hope that the spectroscopic analysis of the Martian atmosphere, taken from Earth, would be to some extent misleading. There was a case for this. The Martian air, though very thin, was a singularly deep and tenuous layer compared with Earth's. The pressure on Earth decreased rapidly with altitude until, at the height of the summit of Everest, it was comparable to the pressure on the Martian surface. Thereafter it still continued to decrease at the same rate. But Mars, starting at that low pressure, had a less steep gradient. The air was thinner, above the surface, but not so much thinner as it would have been on Earth. The curves crossed. The upper air of Mars was comparatively plentiful and extended a long way out. And it was this distant, upper air which had been measured by telescope and spectrograph from Earth.

There was a reasonable probability that air at the surface, which I was now enriching with oxygen and breathing, actually contained more oxygen itself than the mere one per cent which had been forecast by astronomers. But the trouble was, I could not know, when the pressure was so low and the quantities were in any event so small, until I embarked on some sort of fractional analysis.

I began on it that day, and it worried me all night. I was still working on it the next day and the next.

I set up my machine inside the ship. I had to. I had to start with the coldest Martian air I could get. That meant drawing it in at night, and specifically in the pre-dawn hours, when temperatures near the surface dropped to nearly as low a figure as 200° on the Absolute scale, or about, in Fahrenheit notation, a hundred and fifty degrees of frost. I could not work in those temperatures. They had to be kept inside the apparatus I was building.

I got my first step down by drawing the night air through the water-condensation plant. I already had a drop of a good twenty degrees there. I was getting down.

A dozen times I cursed those little pumps from the hydraulic machinery, which was all I had to work with. It is a tough industrial process, to liquefy air and boil off its constituent gases at their respective temperatures. At least, it is if you have not the right equipment.

But if you have enough pumps you can't really go wrong. And I had enough pumps. They were small, they were not intended for the purpose, but they worked. They compressed gases, and that was what I needed.

From the water-condensation tank, the air was drawn in and compressed again. It was fed back through a coil of pipe in the tank, to lose the heat it had gained by its compression. Then it was fed out through a jet into another chamber, becoming colder as it expanded.

I duplicated this refrigerating system, and continued to duplicate it. Each cooling-coil was set in the previous stage's expansion chamber. When I was reaching the end of my resources, I built a box round the whole contraption and filled it with heat-insulation in the form of teased-out blanket. Then I used feed-back, sending the same cold air round the circuit once again.

It was, after all, only the getting of the first, pure drop of liquefied Martian air that was really difficult. After that, I was able to use the unwanted, cold, and almost frozen fluids to cool the earlier stages.

I had five pipes in a row branching off a main pipe along which I maintained a steady, rising slope of temperature. The main pipe was broad, and it dipped and curled. Inside, a bubbling was in progress. No alchemist of ancient times ever approached the results of his experiments so cautiously as I, feeding those cold gases, in small proportions, into my mask.

It was just a fortnight after I landed that I was drinking Martian water and breathing Martian air made by power drawn from Martian sunlight.

That was what really began my troubles: when I realised the possibility of my survival and how much depended on the aggressiveness with which I attacked my problems.

12

FOOD WAS my overwhelming need. I had not thought it would be. The production of air and water in an airless desert had seemed to me so difficult of accomplishment, and so much a near-miracle when it was accomplished, that I had thought the production of food in a place where there was already life of a rudimentary sort to be almost a matter of course.

Was not the desert surrounding the wreck, despite the mean appearance given to it by its narrow, pinched horizons, and the cold and lack of air and water, actually flowering? It was true that the plants were widely scattered and, even supposing I could somehow eat them directly, I would have to range over a wide area to get my food. But they were life, and the human digestion is wonderfully adaptable when it comes to the absorption of living things, and with water —I was getting a little then, and I did not doubt that I would get more in future—I could surely make them grow profusely. Besides, as a last resort, I had the insects and their honey.

I attacked the problem of food with all the energy and directness which I had discovered was necessary if I was to survive. I gave myself an hour's relaxation on the morning after I had solved my immediate air and water problems, and spent it looking at the dun-coloured plain as I emerged from the rocket and at the sky above it, which changed, at different times of day, from dark blue-black to bottle-green. It was a strange sky, which, because the stars were always visible in it except in an area closely around the sun, gave a false impression of nakedness and altitude, but I did not spend too long on it. I was soon doing what I had to do. I went to the nearest of the plants and began gently to ease its spreading, radiating fibres from the dusty earth.

That was where I struck my first difficulty. It was a simple mechanical one. I was down on my knees, examining the plant critically and in detail for the first time, and it only needed my sense of touch to tell me that the apparently fine and succulent red-green tendrils above ground were in fact of the toughness and consistency of leather. I went for the roots, on the assumption that there must be some soft part somewhere. But it would have been more easy to separate the fine filaments of a mushroom root on Earth from the mould in which it grew than to take up and clean the root of that plant. The filaments spread for yards, but, digging in the soil, it was hardly possible to detect them with the naked eye.

The plant came up without its roots, every spreading runner breaking off at the point at which it made contact with the ground.

I was left with perhaps half a pound of tough stems, like a vine on Earth, and with perhaps two ounces of what, because of their green colour, I thought of as the leaves. These, which just conceivably might be edible, were like fine stems of curling grass.

I went back into the wreck. I took my prize into the galley. I prepared a pan of boiling water and put the leaves into it. For a quarter of an hour I watched them boil. Then, very gingerly, I took out one stem and tried to eat it.

It was then that I realised that I was showing more energy than thought. Those leaves were capable of withstanding the great temperature variations of the Martian day and night. And the water I was boiling was not, at that low pressure, at anything like the temperature of boiling water on the surface back on Earth. It was at a comparable, but lower temperature, than the hundred and seventy degrees at which water boiled in the tents of the upper camps of Everest and which had made it impossible for the climbers to brew their tea there. To try to eat that leaf was like trying to eat the toughest, uncooked, frond of grass.

I did not have a pressure cooker. I had to make one from a pan with a tight-fitting lid, which I carefully ground in until I got a perfect fitting on the flange, then loaded with weights until, by the way the steam hissed out, I detected that I had a distinct steam pressure inside. I left the plant to cook in that, at the same time thinking grimly that, if I were to have to use that amount of electric power for every meal, I would soon be back where I started, searching for new sources of energy.

In the meantime I went out of the rocket again, after setting the pan on low heat. It was afternoon by then, but I spent half an hour watching the insects. The singular aspects about them were their methodical distribution, so that I rarely had more than one in my field of view at once, and their habit of travelling in straight lines to and from their nest. They had never taken any notice of the wreck or endeavoured to avoid it or me. I had noticed when I was working on my machines that any obstacle I placed in their way caused them first to draw back, but only for an instant, and then to try to go on over it. If that was impossible—and they lacked both the energy and the adhesion of our quick-climbing species—then they went off at right-angles in a semi-circle, trying again and again with greater diameters of turn until they were able to complete a full semi-circle without deviation from what was evidently for them a geometric course, until they could resume their straight-line path again.

I captured one of the insects and put him in a box. I put the box ready to take with me into the rocket on my return.

Then I did what I hated to do but had to. I took one of the many aluminium bars and pieces which I had had to dismantle from the wreck and walked out to where I had seen the insects' nest. I attacked it with my bar, chipping my way into it from the side. I was wary as I did so, standing back and watching after each few blows. The insects were six inches long as I have said. A creature of the same relative size as myself, attacking an ants' nest back on Earth, would have been attacked in turn and driven off by fighter ants. It was with an expectation of revulsion that I awaited the emergence of the swarm. That the creatures were so slow-moving did not, somehow, lessen the horror that I felt as I imagined breaking through to the inner swarm.

It did not happen. There was something frightening in the very absence of reaction. Those creatures had no responses whatever to attack. While I dug into the side of their nest they came and went with blind indifference. One of them, emerging from their hole, came straight towards me, stopped when he struck my foot, turned, went out in a semi-circle, and then proceeded happily about his business.

When I had the side of the nest open, and could see their roadways and their disgusting grubs, they took no notice. One of them, emerging along a channel that I had broken, fell out of the nest and began to walk in circles. He seemed to have utterly no conception of what had happened to him.

So far as I could see, when night came, they would all die. They were making no immediate effort to rebuild their broken home. I thought about that as I found what I was looking for: a store of greenish liquid in a series of wax-lined cup-like depressions quite near the outside of the nest. I took my sample in an improvised scoop I had brought with me, then carefully built up the nest again. I hoped they would have the sense to reopen the interior channels I had disturbed, but I was not sure. For all I knew, after a million years of stasis, they might die at the slightest disturbance of their way of life. I hoped not. If I found that the honey—I hoped it was that—was all I had to eat, and if a whole nest died each time I took some, I could see myself being forced to adopt a wandering life, and the whole planet would hardly, ultimately, support me.

I went back to the rocket in haste, hoping my pan had not boiled dry. When I arrived I took my specimens in with me, having thought about it first, and tightly enclosed them in lidded boxes. I had been deliberately taking the risk of some strange infection from the Martian air ever since I had first stepped outside my rocket and, though I was beginning to realise that Mars, like the polar regions of Earth, was singularly lacking in infections, I still kept the chances to the minimum.

The pan had not boiled dry. When I took off the lid pale fronds were simmering in a concentrated greenish liquid.

I looked at the result of my handiwork with perturbation.

I wished I had a dog or a cat to try it on. It was true that the brew had not stained the pan, and, so far as I could see, the very greenness, speaking of chlorophyll and the same sort of photo-synthesis by which plants gained their living back on Earth, was reassuring. The boiling should surely have killed bacteria; and the plants, lacking enemies as did the insects, could have had no reason to carry artificial poisons. All the same, I was doubtful. I took a frond in my mouth and held it there, then spat it out, holding a glass of water ready to wash my mouth.

No taste. No result at all at first. Then, faintly, perhaps from the steam that was still arising from the pan, I detected the faint aroma of ammonia.

When I tried again, and bit into a frond, it was distinctly there, faint but repugnant. And there was another taste, which I could not identify. Though I could not identify it, it was enough to cause me to stop my experiments abruptly.

I stood there wondering, then put my pan away. I had so little to go on, no more than smells and flavours. Yet I saw the danger, and a very acute one it was.

I know very little about organic chemistry. But I did know that life on Earth consisted mainly of hydrocarbons with their atoms arranged in certain ways. When the precise construction of the molecules was tampered with no living things resulted but plastics and the innumerable and variegated substances of the chemical industry.

I did not let the devastating knowledge dawn on me just then. I did not dare to. I set to work on my insect. It was unfortunate that I had to kill him with a slender knife, but I had no chloroform nor any of the other equipment of the vivisectionist's table.

As soon as I used the knife, I knew he was not an insect, but of necessity, I had to go on thinking of him as that, because nor was he a vertebrate. He had no external skeleton and no backbone, but only a leathery skin and strips of gristle in his legs.

Outwardly, he consisted of two halves, as opposed to the Earth insect's three sections. His after-part consisted of four legs mounted on an internal structure of gristle that would have served as an excellent model for the fuselage of an aeroplane. His fore-part consisted of a similar structure carrying two legs, his long proboscis, and a pigmented area I took to be an eye.

Inside, the black portion contained what no insect on Earth ever had, a lung. I would be true to say that a good half his weight was lung. It was as though that were the basis of mobile life on Mars: a lung mounted on a means of locomotion. Even the feeding arrangement and diminutive digestive system seemed to be an afterthought. And though I used lenses from the telescopes as my dissection proceeded, I did not find a brain.

It appeared that the eye was the brain. At least, the only thing I could detect resembling a nerve-cord ran to it, with branches throughout the rest of the creature's system.

I hated the job, and as soon as possible I cleared the mess away. It was possible that I might live on Mars on a diet of 'insects'' lungs, but I thought that if I did I would probably die of nausea. If you reached that stage of survival, it was very much a question of why you tried to live at all.

My remaining sample was the honey. And I knew by now that it was not honey, that it originated in a plant that had not the chemistry of an Earth plant, and that it served the needs of a creature that was so unlike anything on Earth that I could not place it in any phylum of biology I had heard of.

It was late by then. As always in the wreck, I was working, in my lonely fashion, beneath the single light bulb, with the cold glitter of metal that had once been functional but now was up-ended in a surrealist fashion all around me. Even to work in the galley I had had to move the stove and stand it upon what had once been the wall partition. My table was the old table-top which had been bolted on to the table legs sideways as they stood out rigidly from what now was wall.

I remembered that Martian honey. I had brought a good supply of it, and first I boiled a little. I still did not dare to touch or taste a thing without boiling first. But this was very different from the faintly ammoniacal steam that had risen from the plants. To describe it is almost impossible. It is easy to speak of an infusion of aromatic herbs, but the mind jumps at once in the wrong directions. The scent that instantly, on the first warming of the pan, filled the interior spaces of the rocket, had nothing to do with thyme or sage nor any of the stranger ingredients that go into Indian curry.

It was alcoholic in the first place. The nearest I can come to a description is to suggest a parallel with a fine liqueur, on the Benedictine pattern.

The substance boiled away, at a very low temperature indeed. It did not even leave a stain on the bottom of the pan.

I found a section of hollow tube that had once been part of the air supply, leading used air back from that compartment to the potassium purification tanks I no longer used. I made a hole in a saucepan lid and inserted the tube and packed the point, bending the tube itself downwards to another container three feet away. I made, in other words, a still. I watched the golden-greenish fluid drip in an oily fashion from the retort.

It was not alcohol. Had it been alcohol, it would have evaporated in daytime heat at the pressure in the rocket. But I tasted it, aware that I was dealing with a substance of largely mineral content.

It was not alcohol, but three drops were enough to give me the heady feeling I was drunk. One drop more, and I knew that my judgment would be so distorted I would drink the lot.

I spent an hour grinning like an idiot and wondering how,

if I ever got back to Earth, I could market my liquor and clean up a fortune before every government banned it.

If it was food, if it could even be described as food, though the quantities I had of it were relatively enormous, it was so dangerous, in its scent and flavour, that I came to think of it as the greatest peril I ran on Mars. Not that it was poisonous in its effects. Not that it even left me with a head. But, drinking it, I would have been sure to sit in idle pleasure while the pumps and machines wore out and the wreck fell in ruin all around me. To say it was habit-forming is a fantastic understatement. It was with a trembling hand and with a determination that I still think of as super-human that I went outside the rocket at midnight in my pressure suit and poured my only available Martian 'food' away. I did not trust myself to live within the scent of it even when I was asleep. I might have sleep-walked, drunk of it, and lived thereafter as a grinning, gibbering idiot, for its chemicals, whatever they were, had an immediate and stupendous effect upon the brain.

Living substances on Mars differed dangerously from their equivalents on Earth.

13

I REMEMBER one of the illustrations in the copy of *Robinson Crusoe* which I read as a boy. Robinson stands on a promontory surveying his island. He wears a goatskin coat and hat, carries his gun over his shoulder, and has his parrot on his arm. Perhaps that is the way a castaway may have looked in those days. I do not know. What I do know is that when I had established myself to the extent of providing myself with the most basic necessities of life for a man of my own age, which was to say air and water and a source of power, and when I had to begin to think of exploring the Martian surface with a view to acquiring the secondary necessities, such as food and a source of raw materials, I must have presented a very different picture.

The tricycle—I remembered my dream—took me a week to make. That it should be made was not dictated by any conception I had of myself as a twentieth-century man, who must automatically possess some form of transport. It was the result of simple observation and necessity. The Martian plain, what I had seen of it, was flat. It seemed to go on for great distances all around me in all directions. To cross it, I must take large supplies of oxygen and water with me, and, even despite the reduced gravity of the smaller planet, I could not envisage myself carrying these necessities, together with shelter for the night, upon my back. Nor did I think that walking would be a fast enough means of progress when I was tied to my base to the extent of having to return to it to replenish my bulky supplies every few days at least.

I thought of it as a tricycle, but it was more like a half-track. The tracks themselves were gear-chains, mounted on gear-wheels, one track on each side of the level platform above the back axles. On Earth, such tracks, made of light unprotected chain, would have rusted through and become immovable as soon as the dust wore off the protective grease. On Mars, owing to the lack of oxygen in the atmosphere, there was no rust.

The tracks were driven by pedals like a bicycle on Earth, or, when the going was tough, the pedals could be assisted by a small electric motor. On Earth the motor would not have been worth taking because of the weight of the battery cells, taken from the wreck, which I used to drive it. On Mars, with the weight of everything cut down to half, it was well worth while. The steering was accomplished by a single wheel at the front, which, with a handlebar and aluminium forks cut from the twisted girder-structure of the wreck, gave the machine its tricycle appearance.

All the machinery came from the gyros and the control-gear of the rocket. The front wheel itself was one of the large, disc-like wheels which, spinning at thirty thousand revolutions a minute, had been the stabilisers of the rocket.

On the level platform at the back of the tricycle I mounted a tank of liquid oxygen. When I was ready to make my first excursion across the plain of Mars, I mounted a seat or saddle above the pedals, took off the harness and cylinder I always had to wear when I moved on foot, and connected my mask to the breathing apparatus mounted on the vehicle. The handlebar was a straight bar, with no fancy curves. I carried not a gun but a telescope slung from my shoulder. On my wrist I carried not a parrot but a compass which I had had to make, beginning by magnetising a piece of iron in a coil of wire.

On the platform behind me, besides the oxygen, were rough boxes containing my equipment. I had only one thing capable of keeping me warm and alive if I had, as I expected, to spend nights out in the open. This was the old pressure suit, which was insulated enough for use in space itself, and which I had to take with me. Apart from that, I had collecting-boxes for the specimens I hoped to find. I had lenses taken from the astronomical telescopes, with which to examine plants and any creatures there might be. I had a hammer, to be used for geological purposes when breaking chips off rocks. I took water and corked bottles.

I also took, inside my own skull, the brain of a twentieth-century man. It had not been a particularly good brain, back on Earth. No one had admired it. No one had ever called me brilliant. I was just the sort of person who was useful on a camping holiday, who would mend his own punctures when out cycling, and who would give a hand to help decarbonise the engine of a car. As a practical engineer, I had never ranked very high with the mathematicians and professors back at Woomera. I had always been more interested in how than why, in whether things looked as though they were going to work rather than in whether they gave me aesthetic pleasure, and even when I had had a phase of intellectualism and taken to vegetarianism as a hobby, I had been more interested in proving to myself that people could live without eating meat than in all the moral reasons that were given for doing it.

14

IN THE COURSE of the next few days I established the geography of my immediate surroundings in the plain. To begin with I was afraid to ride far in any direction lest I lose contact with the wreck and be unable to find it again. The narrow horizons of the desert and its only gently undulating flatness meant that, returning from a one-day's journey of fifty miles—nearly two degrees of latitude by the Martian scale—I might pass within three miles of my base and never see the dull gleam of the broken metal hull which was all I would have to guide me at that distance.

Such a loss of contact with the machines on which I depended for my living would have meant my death within a day, for I could not carry more than forty-eight hours' supply of oxygen with me at that time. I was not content until, by building up girders from the wreck, I had raised a thirty-foot mast above my base, with a flag on top, and then, riding out in all directions, I had established six smaller masts, just out of sight of the main mast, driven into the desert earth and inclined in the direction I must go to regain the centre. Then, I had a target ten miles wide to hit, a circle I could not pass through without the certainty of sighting something, and I felt more confident.

Perhaps such precautions were unnecessary, but no one should decry them who has not themselves felt the awful loneliness, the sense of vacant, inhuman emptiness engendered by that wilderness of Mars. No man, lost on the icy plateau of Tibet, could know the fear of being out of sight of anything on Mars. He would have above him the Earth sky, of cloud and rain and wind. The icy blast, which would tear at his clothes and threaten him with exhaustion by its buffeting would still be breathable air. Lost he might be, but on Earth he would hardly be more than a few hundred miles, a walkable distance, from human kind and sustenance. On Mars, it was true, he would not have to fear the wind, or very rarely, but instead, he would have an awful stillness. He would have, as I had, a sky above him that was itself unearthly, dark or pale green at times, in morning or afternoon, but otherwise a vast hemisphere of deep blue-black, through which, even in daylight, were visible the baleful stars. And even that sky was airless, and the land was populated by creatures which, few in number, would better have not existed for all the use they were to human man, while humanity was millions of miles away—an infinite distance and one quite impassable.

I knew, as soon as I left the wreck at all, that one slip, one mistake, even so small a slip as a twisted ankle, could cause my death. The wreck was my life, my only way of life, and not for a moment, when I was away from it, could I cease to think about how I could get back before the ticking minutes, which used up my oxygen, caused me to die of drowning in the Martian air.

I had made my compass, but I did not know if I could rely on it. It was true that one arm of the needle pointed regularly towards the sun at noon, but I was not aware then that planetary magnetism is a function of a world's rotation. All I knew was that even on Earth early navigators had had difficulties due to the variation of the needle and that on Mars such variations had not been charted and there was no one to do it but myself.

Perhaps there was something ludicrous about my early progress. Before setting off at all, I took specimens of the earth in the immediate vicinity of the wreck, and measured the exact distances between the plants. I counted the number of ants' nests I could see when standing on level ground from one position. Then I rode half a day's journey south, towards the sun (though I could not even be sure of that; it was possible that I was well south of the northern tropic and that the sun was north of me at noon), and took measurements again, on the identical-seeming desert there. Then I rode hastily back to the wreck again, and compared my results with those I obtained by a similar journey north.

There was only a distance of sixty miles between the two positions. On Mars that was a difference of two degrees. It was as though, on Earth, I was trying to determine the geography of the planet by measuring the distance apart of similar trees, growing in similar conditions, in places as far away as Manchester and London.

But I had faith in the regularity of Mars. I knew that while on Earth weather had more effect than climate, on Mars vegetation swept southward from the pole in the Northern summer, due, I imagined, to the melting of the polar cap and the liberation of water vapour into the air. Or perhaps I did not know it. Perhaps it was only a hypothesis of mine. But, of necessity, I was not a theoretical scientist, demanding that facts be gathered and assembled before a conclusion could be drawn from them. As a practical man, I had to guess what facts might be important, which meant I had to make my hypothesis first, in order to decide what I had to look for.

The average spacing of plants around the wreck was one of five yards and one foot in all directions. The plants grew to a maximum of three inches high and their roots spread out, above ground, to a distance of two feet six inches. To the south, the distance between the plants was the same, and so was their height and their circumference, but their appearance differed. They looked somehow, strangely, thinner on the ground. To the north, the average distribution was one plant in less than each five yards. Their circumference was narrower, but they grew to four inches high. The ants' nests, as I called them, were distinctly more frequent in the north.

I decided to make my first journey, my first long journey with an all-night camp, to the north. It was possible that I was being misled. The insects and the flowering plants were desert fauna and flora. Perhaps I would only be going deeper into the desert. Perhaps, indeed, my 'south' was north. But only experiment could decide. I had reached that stage of my knowledge of the Martian terrain: I was ready for the experimental testing of my hypothesis.

I set off at dawn, when the slanting sun-rays somehow reflected from the upper atmosphere and caused it to take on that pale-green hue, like a faintly perceptible fluid in which the unwinking stars still seemed to swim. It was cold, dreadfully cold, at that hour on the Martian surface, and at that hour, though I doubt if I would have talked much to a companion if I had had one—it would hardly have been possible while wearing masks—I missed companionship most keenly. I discovered an awful fact: that though it may be difficult to leave good friends and plunge into the unknown, it is even more difficult when you have no friends to leave and no one to watch you go.

I took a slightly different route from the one I had taken on my previous half-day passage. It was thus that I passed an area where there were no plants at all, while away to the right of me was a drift of sand. I stopped for a moment to gain my breath and look at it. It was only sand, and should have been disheartening. But any change in that endless landscape was an improvement to me then. I went to the sand and took a specimen. Even common sand might have its uses. If it was pure sand, I might make glass with it. . . . I remounted and rode on.

By noon, the sand was gone, and I stopped to take measurements of the plants. They agreed with my previous jottings. My sense of expectation grew. In the direction in which I was travelling there seemed to be a regular increment of growth, not merely a local improvement due to some difference in the surface.

But first, before pressing on, I had to eat, and that was a difficult and dangerous business. I had tried, once, to breathe the Martian air. My mind had become hazy and drunken, with all the symptoms of anoxia, and I had hardly had sense enough to replace my mask. I had learned that while the Martian air was not in the slightest dangerous of itself—I breathed it all the time when mixed with oxygen in my mask—it was deceptive. The body struggled for breath, yet seemed to be breathing normally. So now, sitting behide my machine on the desert earth, beneath the blue-black noonday sky which shone with stars all around the horizon's edge though the sun was overhead, I cautiously took off my mask after taking a breath, drank of the water I had brought with me, and replaced my mask again. Eating was even more difficult, when I had to chew, yet the whole process had to be gone through carefully.

I sat on for five minutes after eating. I wished I had someone to talk to once again. It was not for the sake of companionship this time, but because, by talking, I could have expected to clear my mind about what, if anything, I hoped to find. Man, I thought grimly, is a talking animal. That is how his mind works: by words and expressed concepts which make his experiences become real and have meaning for him. Without words, without talk about what he sees and thinks, he is little better than the brutes. Then I remounted and rode on once more.

Previously, I had been able to make a straight track across the waste. The plants had rarely come directly beneath my wheels, and when they had, I had not noticed them. They had been too thin to cause a bump. Now, I could not help but run over them, they were perceptibly so much thicker on the ground, and when I did so there was not so much a bump as a slight squelch. I was thankful that the plain was not too stony. My improvised saddle was not too comfortable, and I had not been able to fit my machine with springs. And now, in the afternoon, I sweated as I rode.

The distance I could cover by nightfall would be my total distance. At dawn the following day, I would have to turn back in order to return to the rocket before the succeeding night.

It must have been at about three p.m. that I noticed that the plants were becoming a definite obstacle to my progress. I do not think, such was the toil of my travelling, that I noticed what was happening immediately. It was the chance of passing near one of the now all-too-frequent ants' nests that stopped me. I noticed not so much something new as an absence of what there had been.

The strange creatures which I called ants had always been visible until that moment. Always, around the nests, I had seen them coming and going and I had been to some pains not to run over them as I passed. Now, I remembered that I had not seen them for some time. And, seeing the nest from above, I saw that its opening, the hole or door at the top which the workers used, was closed.

I stopped and stared at the nest. It was, indubitably, of the same type as before, of the same pyramidal shape and made, as they all were, of the unchanging desert earth. But the hole had been plugged and the mound was lifeless.

I looked around me at the plants. Was it connected or disconnected that they seemed to have lost their flowers? Though, in this comparatively lush region of the desert, I had earlier seen double blooms, now such flowers as there were were faded, with fallen petals. Ahead of me, the desert stretched green, not pink or mauve.

I rode on for perhaps half an hour, then stopped again. The plants, flowerless, were one foot high, and I was toiling through them. But it was not that which stopped me. It was the sight, on the top of one of the plants, of a green, round fruit.

The ants were in hibernation—though the word, so far as I could guess, referred to the wrong season—and yet there was a fruit.

I remembered how, on seeing the flowers, I had thought: Flowers for what? Then I had seen the ants.

It was two hours later, and almost on the evening of my advance into the region of the Martian summer, that I pushed my progress so far as to see the first ripe fruit. It was large and tough and leathery, like a cactus. It was about a foot in diameter and two feet high.

It would have been taller still, perhaps four feet or so, except that it had been bitten clean in half.

Yet when I tried to cut it with my knife, the skin was as tough as my leather shoe sole.

15

I REMEMBER another picture of my famous precursor in the art of lonely living. He stands on the empty beach of his earthly island, looking downwards and wearing an expression of fear and disconcertment. And what causes his strained attitude, he who until that moment had had nothing to hope or fear, is a naked human footprint in the sand.

So I must have stood, looking at that bitten cactus-fruit. It was the fruit for which I had perhaps been looking, which might, just conceivably might, yield to some treatment which might turn it into human food. But, in the moment of finding it, as a part of finding it, I became aware that I was not alone.

I had simply not believed in large-scale life on the planet Mars. That there could be other creatures of even remotely animal nature had seemed as impossible to me as that an Abominable Snowman should dwell on the upper reaches of the mountains in Tibet. It had been an unlikely fiction, not sustainable on any practical grounds at all.

Yet on Earth the wildest tundra supported reindeer. There were great creatures, polar bears and whales, which sustained themselves at the very poles. Our Earth deserts supported such outlandish creatures as the camel, the llama, and the yak. If there was no animal life at Everest's summit, it was not due to altitude or cold but because the gales and snow and ice had reduced the land to naked rock.

While I, as I looked away from the fruit and quickly all about me, saw I was in a fruiting desert now. I was on the very rim of the planet's summer, and ahead of me the land was tinged with red and gold.

The red and gold had been seen from Earth. We had said that because there was so little oxygen in the atmosphere only the lowest plants could grow there. But perhaps even in that we had been guilty of confusion in our own minds. We men on Earth judged all things by ourselves. We put the camel as a lower form of life than the higher apes, although, unquestionably, it was a more highly adapted form.

Higher life, lower life, I thought, looking at that reddish, yellow-cored, bitten fruit: what did we judge them by, intelligence? If we did, then biology was not a science. That life was 'highest', if such a term could be used at all, which had adapted itself farthest from the sea of chemical syrups which had borne it.

For it came to me instantly, as I stared unbelievingly at that sliced fruit, that I was not the 'highest' life on Mars. On the contrary, I was a highly ill-adapted being. I lived with difficulty and by machines. I was no better adapted to survive on Mars than was a child on Earth that had been stricken by infantile paralysis and confined to an artificial lung.

It took all my will-power to restrain myself from the urge to leap back upon my machine, to turn it round, and to ride back, at all speed, into my naked, open desert. For a creature that could slice through a fruit like that must be formidable in the extreme—formidable if only because of the size to which it had grown, as it must have grown, on a planet with half the gravitational force of Earth.

I forced myself to stand and think. My eyes had, after all, assured me that there was nothing visible within the confines of my horizon. And I knew, realizing what the rapid change in the desert meant, that it was no use to flee.

The desert near the wreck had been, since I had landed on it, a vacancy of sparsely flowering plants. The plants there would always remain sparse. Their distribution could not change as the season advanced. But they could, and must, develop as these plants had developed. They were, when I had left them, still in the stage of spring and blossom. They were still being pollinated by the 'insects'. But they must, soon, begin to fruit like these. And then, if creatures lived on the fruits, and moved southwards in the bearing season. . . .

I had not once thought, since I had seen the plants around the wreck, what fruit they bore. I had been satisfied with the simple relationship between the plants and the insects, not considering that on Earth no relationships were so simple. As well might I have seen an apple tree in bloom and thought that the tree and the bees which hummed around it were the finished picture, without a thought of birds. Or I might have seen a field of corn and not predicated man!

I looked quickly around me again as some half-formed thought slipped through my mind, and then I resumed my staring at that fruit. The thoughts were welling up in me so swiftly that half of them were lost and only the more consistent, dominant ones, remained with me and registered on my memory.

I could have guessed that there would be other creatures. Even Earth astronomers, once convinced that there was plant life on the planet, could have done so. Perhaps there had been an unsuspected innocence in all our thinking about such matters. Planets with little oxygen in the air, we had thought, could not bear animals. Mars could have none, and nor could Venus, because her atmosphere seemed to consist largely of carbon dioxide!

We had once thought, on similar *a priori* reasoning, that the sun revolved around the Earth.

There, contemplating that bitten fruit on Mars, I thought suddenly in new terms of our cosmos. I thought of Earth as a well-watered planet on which vegetation thrived and was the dominant form of life. *That* was what the quantity of oxygen in the Earth atmosphere meant—not that ours was a planet greatly suited to animal and human life but that the oxygen-breathing animals could not keep pace with the oxygen-exhaling plants. On Venus, it would be the other way. If 'animal' life consisted only of bacteria, still, there, it must be the dominant form, and plants, though growing in conditions which might be perfect for them, would still be the rarer types, eaten, probably, as soon as they appeared. And on Mars?

Oxygen was rare in the atmosphere, as I knew too well. There was, I had already discovered, an excess of carbon dioxide over it.

I looked round fearfully, then back at the fruit again. I looked round once more, at the gently rolling plain that was in my view, then back once more. I had the evidence before me and I knew, both from the light gravitational attraction of the planet, and from the thinness of the air, that if creatures there were, besides myself, they must have grown to gargantuan size, with long and slender bones, great bellow-like lungs, and jaws that could slice such a fruit in half.

I turned at last, at last conquering the flood of thoughts that battled through my brain. I did what I might have done whole minutes sooner. I looked not at the fruit but at the ground besides the plant, to the earth that was trodden by my footsteps, but which might bear the imprint of another.

I saw it there, the elongated impression, as of a giant's shoe-sole.

I moved beyond the plant. The earth was disturbed beside it and for some little distance northwards. Then, by impressions in the ground, and from the trodden, broken roots of plants, I inferred that a two-legged creature had come rapidly from north-eastwards, stopped at the plant, and then moved back north-westwards. Heaven knew that I was no tracker, but the impressions were unmistakable, as unmistakable as footprints on a shore.

And I had not made them. I did not make weighty footprints three yards apart. What I did not know was whether the creature that had made them was man, or bird, or beast.

16

BEFORE SUNSET, I moved five more miles back into the still unfruiting desert, and there I camped. I had thought, previously, of the difficulties and dangers of this camp in the open on the Martian surface. I had brought the pressure suit to wear as insulation against the cold, and a tiny tent or covering in which I could lie beside my machine on open ground. I had wondered, seriously if that would be enough, and whether I could survive.

But now it was not the cold I feared.

The cold, indeed, was less than I expected. I have mentioned the dew which was the only irrigation of that whole vast plain, but now, so near the summer belt of life, the dew settled down from nightfall onwards with almost the proportions of a soaking mist. As, with my gloved hands, I touched the fabric of the narrow tent above me, made as it was from bunk-sheets from the wreck, I felt it tight and drumlike, and, through the foreplate of my helmet, I saw that it was translucent with the light of one or other of the moons of Mars.

I had retired into the tent at sundown, remembering my cautious fears of the cold of night. I had allowed my pressure suit partially to inflate, to give me that extra pressure which I knew would help me to guard against the cold. But now, within an hour, I moved to go out again into the Martian night. For one thing, the cold did not seem to be happening in that location and at that season. At least the dew was settling and not yet freezing. And, for another thing, I had more to fear than cold.

It was difficult to get out of that narrow tent in my clumsy pressure suit. I lay for a while with only my head out, looking up at the stars which looked, now it was night, too like the same stars seen from Earth. It was some time before I realised what it was. They were winking, as stars do when shining through the heavy atmosphere of Earth. It must have been the mist, and the temperature gradations which must exist in the upper reaches of the thin but deeply layered atmosphere of the smaller planet. Then, turning my head, I saw one small moon almost right above me and another setting in the west. I struggled out and to my feet.

There was a stillness. I was used to stillness. It was the greatest and most lonely feature of the plain around the wreck. I had often thought that I had never known silence until I came to Mars.

But why had I come out? It had not been to admire the view nor to undergo the experience of seeing two moons in the sky at once. Nor had it been simply because I could not sleep, my mind being too active and far too full of thoughts. I had moved, instinctively, into the little space between my tent and my machine, and now I looked slowly, turning carefully so as not to make any sound, around the whole horizon.

It was empty, as empty as it had always been and as I had

known it would be and yet had found reason to assure myself that it would be. Mars, I told myself, was not a planet for nocturnal creatures. The mist was heavy now, clinging and just faintly visible in the moonlight on the surface, but by dawn the plain would be covered with a layer of frost.

Since I could not sleep, I walked to and fro a little. Tomorrow, I must go back to the wreck. I dared not delay, even moved as I was by the conflicting motives of curiosity and fear. I had brought a sample of the fruit, but I had not dared to taste it yet. Too much depended on my getting back to where I came from to risk the slightest physical disability on the way.

Even if the fruit were edible, it was still not a good prospect for me to try to live on it exclusively, as I would have to do when my store of food ran out. And it might not be edible. I did not see how it could be when the plants it came from had that ammoniacal flavour which marked the difference of their chemistry from anything we had on Earth.

Almost despite myself, I found myself thinking of the creature that had sliced the fruit, and made the footprints, in terms of game. If I only knew more about it! It might, for all I knew, be the highest form of life on Mars. It might be, to some degree, intelligent. . . .

What was I thinking of? I turned and paced my way back to my tent again after twenty yards. Cows and bulls and the farmyard beasts of Earth were intelligent to some degree: to a higher degree, probably, than anything I was likely to find on this barren planet. And man ate them because he had to. Was I thinking my way back into my old, incredibly distant, vegetarian crankiness on Earth? Heaven knew, I had outgrown that long ago. I never had been convinced of the moral reasons for vegetarianism. It had not seemed reasonable or just to me that man should kill off all his domestic animals, and turn the world into one vast cornfield, merely because he did not like to eat the flesh of the creatures which, while he was omnivorous, he could at least allow to live. No, it was not that.

It was something far more basic. It was the dimly dawning knowledge that if I were to live on Mars I must come to some terms with my environment. I must fit in with it, if only as a predator. But no creature, even one from another planet, could succeed as a predator, as a killer of what he found, unless he were equipped with adequate means for his defence.

I turned again, and once more walked my twenty yards across the plain, needing to move now in order to keep warm. I had not thought, until that afternoon, that I might need weapons on this planet. I had thought of myself as a lone creature in a wilderness where my main need was to construct. I had thought that I would learn and thereby discover how to fabricate a way of living. But life was not and never had been like that. For any creature living in any environment where there was any other life at all the art of destruction was a prime necessity.

So I would go back tomorrow—today it almost was—and, before I ventured on to the fruiting plain again, or before the plants in my own locality came to fruit, I would equip myself, if only with a bow and arrow.

Peace came to my mind when I decided this. I did not think that, by deciding it, I had evaded my plain duty to myself to learn all I could while I was in the locality frequented by the creatures. I did not think that I had done what a myriad of foolish men before me had also done, decided that destruction was the easier way. I thought, indeed, that I could sleep, and I turned to my tent to do so, hoping to get my rest despite the discomfort of my pressure suit.

While in my pressure suit, I could only see forward through a narrow arc. It was thus not until I turned that I saw it.

It was a light, a moving light, on the horizon to the westwards.

I stood rigidly, and yet it was only the stiffness of the pressure suit that prevented me falling to my knees. I looked and looked again. I closed my eyes and opened them. I tried to imagine that it was a star, or even some phosphorescent Martian glow-worm at some nearer distance. Certainly it was a green, unearthly radiance.

Then it turned and flashed at me, and I saw it was a narrow beam.

I dropped then, suddenly, to my hands and knees. A moment later, I pressed myself down upon the earth. For the light appeared to be coming in my direction before it passed along the horizon and disappeared on my right.

Yet it was not because of the light that I remained flat then, with my helmet pressed down upon the earth. It was because, in that position, sounds came to me, as a tremor through the ground. I had heard nothing through the attenuated air, but sound travelled more readily through the earth.

I do not know what I would have expected to hear, had I known that I would hear sounds at all. On seeing the light, my mind had filled with wild imaginings. I had thought of vehicles, of men, or at least of man-like creatures, of civilisation, of roads, of cities.

But the sound that came to me through my helmet and the earth was that of stamping, of the elephantine movement of some great beast, which first became louder, then faded, and finally died away into the distance.

17

THREE HOURS later, I was on my way. I did not wait for dawn, but started in my pressure suit when my watch assured me that the first light would appear in half an hour.

I drove southwards, urgently, to the wreck, to make what preparations I might for the coming southward surge of life.

I drove across the desert that day as though I felt the hot breath of Martian life behind me, overtaking. I was weary and sleep-dogged after my restless night and my energy of the day before. I had not understood that though I had acclimatised well to the 'altitude' of the Martian air, and though I breathed, while riding, an atmosphere that was three parts oxygen to one of the inert gases of the atmosphere, yet sustained effort was almost impossible to me. By noon, while I toiled under the full, unfiltered sunlight, I guessed that I was hardly more than half-way there, despite my early start.

Never had the desert seemed more endless, more interminable, more desiccated, barren, featureless, and utterly lonely, than it did that afternoon.

Towards sunset, I began to believe that I had lost my way. One thing I had lost, with certainty, was my outward tracks, which, faint though they were across the dusty, stony surface, I had been following earlier. And if I were lost, if I did not find the wreck by sunset, my condition would be serious. I would not be completely lost. By economising on oxygen through the night, I might still be alive by morning and have enough air left to search for another half-hour after dawn. But I could not believe I would do that. I could not believe that I would rest through the night knowing what would depend on that half-hour when morning came. Instead, I would be tempted to wander on, to search by chancy moonlight, use up my air by breathing heavily, as I was already doing throughout that lengthy afternoon.

When the sun was actually on the horizon, I despaired. I made one last desperate rush in the direction which my compass said was south. And, five minutes later, I sighted the easternmost outpost I had set up to guide me back. Either some unsuspected deviation of the compass had upset me—I suspected the magnetism of my machine itself must cause an alternate deflection whether it faced north or south —or in my weariness my steering had been erratic. I did not find the strength to wonder which. I turned in the direction in which I now knew with certainty that the wreck must lie, and arrived there just as final darkness settled down.

I slid through the airlock and took refuge in the sweet Earth-sanity of the interior of the rocket with much the same feelings a dog must have when he finds safety behind his master's gate. I was too tired to eat, but I drank two pints of fresh, clear water and lay down on my improvised couch in the control compartment. I expected to fall asleep immediately and to awake in the morning with a clearer conception of what had happened.

Instead I lay awake, with the light on, and looked about me at the metal walls of the wrecked ship that was my home. In those moments when my overtired, fevered brain lay battling with the unknowns of Mars, I had a clearer conception of myself and of my position on the planet than any I had had since I had landed.

The steel shell which covered me, which provided me with shelter and air and water—that was not Mars. I had only to turn my head and see couches, instruments, pipes and electric leads which had been made on Earth. So far, that was what I had worked with. All my puny striving on this planet had not been a conquest of Mars but only improvisation, with Earth equipment, to fit me for a strange environment.

Mars was stranger, greater, and more unknown than I had imagined that it could be.

I had been a fool. I had been in the position of a creature from another planet who had landed on Earth and chanced to make first contact with the surface on the frozen wastes of Lapland. Seeing the moss, the lichens, and stunted grasses, he would assume that that was all the life there was. Then he would be confronted, as the season advanced, with a herd of reindeer. Or I was one who might have landed on

Earth's Sahara. In a wilderness of sand and thorny scrub, he would have despaired of higher life until suddenly he came upon a camel.

So I, on my first journey outside my shell, had come across the footprints of some two-footed creature, and seen a light and heard the sound of ponderous movement in the night. What now of my belief that Martian creatures must necessarily be unintelligent and slow-moving, that with so little oxygen in the air to breathe, they would only be able to sustain their body temperatures in the heat of day, and that brains could not develop without the fuel and air and precise temperature control which animals and birds achieved on Earth? I had thought those things.

But now I was not so sure. On Earth, the human body had adapted itself to sustain wide temperature variations in the world around it. Other creatures, such as polar bears, were more adapted. Herbivorous animals on Earth had multiple stomachs, to enable them to deal with the coarsest grasses. Why not, on Mars, creatures with multiple lungs, with lights like deep-sea fish—or even with intelligence of some sort that was totally alien to myself?

I fell asleep at last, shaken and fearful, and by no means as sure of myself as I had been. I dreamed that when the summer wave of life which swept twice yearly across the Martian surface reached my broken rocket the desert around me teemed with forms of life which, if I had not dreamed them, would have been undreamable.

18

WHEN I LOOKED at my watch again it was noon or midnight. In the interior of the rocket I could only tell if it were day or not by turning to look at the half-buried window. It was day, and it must be noon. I got up, and as I moved about inside my shelter it seemed to me that a shade that I was coming to know too well was looking over my shoulder once again.

When Crusoe had discovered that savages were in the habit of visiting his island, he had enlarged his cave and improved the stockade he had built around it. He had feared the unknown inhuman humans. What I did, that very afternoon, was to tear out wiring from the rocket, strip insulation from it, and take it out into the desert. On metal stakes driven into the earth I hung it around the rocket at a radius of twenty yards. Then I ran two insulated leads back to the battery. I found, in the smashed electronic equipment, a transformer. I worked to make a trembler coil and used the transformer to step up the voltage. With the trembler in operation, and with five hundred volts on the wire, I felt I could sleep more securely behind my electric fencing than Crusoe ever could behind his stockade.

Then I went inside again and looked at a specimen of the fruit that I had brought back with me. If there was to be food for me on Mars, then this, or some derivative from it, must be it.

I had some knowledge of the scientific method. I knew the principles that permeated all science, whether botany, biology, or medicine. Experiments must be made in controlled conditions, in which one feature only could be unknown. I was careful therefore to eat nothing and to drink only pure water. Then, gingerly, I tasted the fruit.

At least it did not have the flavour of ammonia, but it was acid as no Earth fruit was ever acid, and bitter, and quite uneatable as it stood. The texture and colour of the flesh beneath the leathery skin was not unlike a melon.

The flavour was such that I was not surprised, when I boiled a portion of the fruit in my aluminium pan, to discover that it etched and stained the surface of the metal. I certainly could not eat it as it was.

I went to my medicine chest and took out the expedition's supply of bicarbonate of soda. It took a teaspoonful to neutralise a saucepan full of the acid fruit. The substance that was left was salty but edible. I watched myself carefully for some hours afterwards, but I felt no ill effects and my hunger seemed to be appeased, though I had acquired a thirst.

I felt baffled. Though I would shortly have, in the desert around me, an unlimited supply of the fruit for food, I had by no means an unlimited stock of bicarbonate of soda. Not only was the quality of the food extremely poor but I would very rapidly run out of the wherewithal to treat it.

Among my remaining stores had been a few cans of milk. One of these I had opened before I went away on my expedition. Since then, it had gone bad and begun to grow a mould, but, in my lonely bachelor fashion, I had not emptied nor thrown away the tin. I had, of necessity, to try everything. I put small cubes of the fruit on plates around the galley. Some, I simply left unprotected. Others I covered with water and left there to ferment. One, I infected with the milk, and still another I touched with a scraping of the mould.

I wished I knew more about yeasts and bacteria. I wished I knew exactly what I was doing, but I did not. All I knew was that savages in many parts of Earth made the most poisonous fruits and roots edible by processes such as I was trying to invent.

Finally, to complete the work of that short day, I went out beneath the pale green sky of the Martian evening and examined the plants carefully in the immediate vicinity of the wreck. I saw now, having seen what to expect farther north, that their flowers were fading. Beneath the petals as they dropped and fell, hard bulbs were forming. I looked for the insects, but I did not see a single one. When I went to their near-by nest, the one I had tapped for their dangerous honey, I discovered that the top was sealed. I went back to the wreck thoughtfully, deciding that summer was on its way.

Since I had still felt no ill effect from my eating of the

fruit, I allowed myself to make and eat a normal meal. During it, I tried to puzzle out the question of the seasons.

It had been seen from Earth how the wave of life on Mars started from each pole in turn, following the melting of the ice cap. Some confusion had arisen among astronomers from this fact. At first, it had been thought that this melting of the snows, followed by an expanding wave of life, gave some substance to the theory of the canals, as though Mars were some vast Egypt, where irrigation made the desert flower.

I knew better now. I knew that the moisture was dispersed through the Martian atmosphere as a spreading mist. As, on Earth, comparatively small variations in the sun's power and heat had caused vast ice ages and interregnums, due to the alternate locking up and releasing of water from the icefields of the poles, so on Mars, with its longer year, each hemisphere might be said to have an annual ice age. Mist freezing on the desert where I was would melt each day all the year round. But in the polar regions in winter the ice would not melt but would accumulate, not as snow but as layer upon layer of frost. By the equinox, the air of the planet would be dry.

Then would come the melting of the other polar cap. Those scientists were right who said that water, in its free state, could not exist on Mars, but would evaporate and diffuse itself through the upper atmosphere as it did through the stratosphere on Earth. Yet each night would cause a condensation and a mist, and so, beginning near the pole, and not near the equator as on Earth, the wave of life would sweep across the Martian surface once again. The plants around me in the desert were in this stage. They had grown from the nightly dews, they had spread their wide net of roots, and flowered, and fed the insects and been pollinated by them. Now, for a short period, they would come to their fruition.

But plants did not produce fruit needlessly or uselessly.

Fruit was an attraction for creatures which took it and disseminated the seed. My creatures. Great creatures which had to be huge in size for two reasons.

One reason was what I had already thought of: that the gravitational attraction of a smaller planet demanded a larger structure for its creatures. It was strange to think of, but none the less scientifically inescapable that a large planet could bear only thick-legged, stunted dwarfs, because no strength of material could support the weight of a taller body against a powerful gravitational attraction, while Mars, or Earth's moon, once vegetation was established, would permit giraffe-like creatures the size of elephants.

The moon was barren, but Mars was not, and the conclusion I came to was startling, though it had been staring me in the face.

It was not that Martian life could be very, very large, but that it would have to be. Unless, like the plants, Martian mobile life hibernated for eighteen Earth-months every year, it would, of necessity, have to follow the wave of life. It would start at one pole, with the melting of the snows, follow the wave of life down to the equator and across it. Then, for three months, it would have to fast and trek slowly down to the other pole, there to await the new life-wave which would sweep up the path the last one had swept down.

Large creatures carry or nurture their young for a longer period. On Earth, with a twelve-month year, the variations of the seasons put a premium on the size of growth represented by men and cows and sheep and other annual-bearing species. On Mars, the 'natural' size would be twice as large. And the need to trek great distances across the planet would give advantage to an even larger size.

Having thought of that, of the natural explanation for what I had seen on my northward journey, and surveying the remains of the first good meal I had eaten in three days, I felt well satisfied. Not even the depressing, metallic surroundings of the rocket could dim my reviving spirits. The fact that I too, if I were to survive on Mars, would have to learn to follow the wave of life, and adopt a nomadic existence on the desert, seemed to me to be just another matter to be taken in my stride. Had I not found a possible source of food? And was I not likely to find edible game just so long as I kept up with the stream?

I got up and looked at my squares of fruit. Two were unchanged, one was fermenting busily, and another had changed colour and gone quite white.

I tasted the white one gingerly. Not even with all will and wish in the Martian world could I say that it tasted pleasant. But I managed to eat a tiny portion of it, and again I did not collapse writhing with stomach pains.

19

HE WAS crossing the plain like some legendary giant. I looked up when I was working outside the wreck, and there he was, coming in towards me from the north-eastwards, striding slowly, well within the pinched horizon of the plain under the thin Martian sunlight and the pale green sky.

I had made a bow, a very good bow with a steel shaft and a wire string and alloy arrows tapped and screwed into iron barbs. It was lying two paces from where I worked, but I froze and did not go to it.

It was a shock to see that his shape was vaguely man-like. I ought not to have been startled by that fact, despite his size. I should have thought that that general shape, with a body mounted on two legs, and with two appendages for use as arms, had been so successful on Earth that it was at least probable that some creature would be endowed with the same equipment on any other planet bearing life. But it was not his similarities to a man but his differences that appalled me. And yet his actions had a purposefulness that was almost human.

He came forward in bursts or periods of walking of about a hundred yards. At first, such was my own immediate and animal reaction, I thought he was stalking me. I watched him without appearing to watch him, ready, this time, to learn what I could before I indulged in flight or self-defensive action. Then I realised that he was making no attempt at self-concealment, not even during the periods of not-walking, when, had he been stalking in Earth-fashion, he would have frozen to absolute motionlessness. He moved and did something during those times when he was stopped, and I realised that, far from stalking me, he was utterly oblivious of me and was taking no notice either of myself, or of the rocket, or of all that scattered wreckage which lay around, incontestable but hardly explicable to him, over a quarter-mile area of his Martian plain.

I moved then. I went quickly to my bow and took up a position immediately behind a large tank or vat that I had been making with the idea and hope of collecting the fruit when it ripened in my area and storing it and processing it and turning it into food. But he paid no attention to my motion any more than he had to my stillness. He too was interested in the fruit: that was the next thing that registered with me. When I saw what he was doing I thought instantly of that isolated sample of the fruit I had seen away in the north, that had been sliced, or bitten, clean in half.

He was a quarter-mile away from me now, and still coming forward. Every hundred yards he stopped and bent forward the pale blue barrel-shape of his body. His arm made a circular motion as though to strike a blow. It was the fruit he touched, or picked, or sliced: I could see that. But then, after an instant's pause, he performed what I can only describe as a little dance. He took a pace or two forward and another back and seemed to trail a leg. I watched him with a puzzlement that was overlaid by a growing fear.

I did not know if I were going to be able to live off the products of the plain. I did know that if I were going to win my harvest and garner it I would have to contest an area, a territory, with whatever creatures the slowly softening climate brought down to me from the north. And here was the first, unknown and with all the menace of the unknown, doing *something* within the territory, which I must establish as my own.

The onus was on me to attack. If 'he' was as oblivious and incurious of me as he seemed to be, then it was I who would have to drive him off. But I was not, in this situation, the Modern Man, with a gun in his hand and all the power and might of an unchallengeable civilisation behind him. Instead I was a lonely, puny, diminutive creature whose weapon—the bow I held now—was itself a symbol not of strength but weakness. I was one of my kind—and ignorant.

I went forward to the limit of my wire. The creature took no notice of me. It was typical of what I now regarded as his mystery that he was not coming straight towards me but rather on a course which would take him within a hundred yards of me and past. I could not conceive of any creature on Earth that would pass so near to an utterly strange and alien feature in its environment and not pause or hesitate or draw back and look, yet this Thing did none of those things. He came on and I saw he was monstrous now: twenty feet tall and slow, and yet inexplicably dainty in his movements. I wondered if I should go outside my wire—I would have to do that if I were going to attack—and I wondered if, were I to attack and be defeated, I would be able to get back again and switch on the electric current which I regarded as my only real defence.

I knew in my mind that I ought not to go out. I ought to watch and then, maybe, later, follow. But, at the same time, I found it impossible to be strictly logical. The Thing was there, and if I did not face it then, how would I face it later when it came back, perhaps with half a dozen others, perhaps with half a hundred or a horde? I pulled a switch which I had set near the perimeter of the wire for just this purpose, unhooked a section, and stepped through. I had never understood before how it is that fear drives a man forward to attack, but now I knew.

I went into the path of the creature, and he came on towards me. My hand was on my bow and I felt an almost irresistible urge to shoot. It took all my intelligence to restrain myself from attempted murder until I had exhausted every other course. For the Thing had eyes—nature had so far repeated herself as to endow him with binocular vision —and, for the first time, I saw them fixed on me as he approached at a distance of a hundred yards.

Approached, and kept on coming, huge and bulbous, with a strangely mincing gait. As he towered up towards me I looked back quickly at the way I would have to run, saw the gap in my wire open and the switch ready to make it impassable to any creature I could know or understand, and then I picked up a stone and threw it.

I missed. It whistled past his head. And he kept on coming, I imagined, threateningly. Desperately, my hand went to my bow again, but then I rejected it and picked up another stone. I was dimly aware that my purpose was not to declare open war but merely to drive him off. I threw again and hit him square in the middle of what I can only describe by calling it his face.

He came on. He was damaged. I saw an injury to his eye. It was too late to fire my bow now. I turned from his path and ran.

He went on, straight past me. I turned stupidly and stared. Within twenty yards of me, and presenting a perfect target for my bow, he stopped. He leant forward. With a swipe of his arm, he severed half an unripe fruit. He lifted it to his head and seemed to taste it. He dropped it and began what I had thought of as his dance. Now I saw that what he did was to make a mark, with his foot, upon the ground. Then he altered his course to the westwards and went on.

I followed in his tracks. Wildly I looked around the whole horizon. There was nothing else to be seen. Except for this one incomprehensible creature the plain was as it had been ever since I had landed on it. Crazily, I tried to remember my experiences on the night I had spent out in the north. I remembered the lights, the great beast stamping, and then I looked at the back of the Thing before me.

The memory and the actuality did not fit. I was not now looking at the thing I had seen and heard. But I was looking at the one that had cut the fruit. I saw as I passed the one I had seen him cut that it looked the same exactly as the fruit I had seen in the evening in the north. I do not know which thought compelled me most: the knowledge that I was not dealing with a single species or the fact that this Thing, whatever it was, now seemed to me strangely dumb and senseless.

I had thought that any creature on Mars must have the same reactions that were common to all Earth species. It must know pain and fear and aggression. If it were intelligent, it must have curiosity. If it were not, it must have courage or its equivalent. But, as I looked at the great barrel back of the retreating creature, I could make nothing of it except that it had a blind, decisive purpose. It went to another plant and treated it as it had the first, and then it turned north-west abruptly, with me on its tail, wondering.

It seemed to me that it had tried the fruit in the vicinity of the wreck, discovered that it was not yet ripe, and now was retreating northwards.

I do not know why I drew my bow. I think it was the same instinct for self-assertion which makes small boys watch insects for a while, ants perhaps as they cross the road, and then either stamp on them or try to injure them and attempt to stop their flow. It is one of the less admirable of human traits: a desire to use power, or to try power for power's sake. But, standing behind the Thing as he stopped again, I fitted an arrow to my bow, drew back the string, and fired.

I had practised sufficiently to hit a target seven feet wide at a distance of twenty yards. My arrow flew true. It hit the pale blue and apparently fleshy body. It must have hurt, too, for, for the first time, I saw the creature quiver.

But the sharpened arrow-tip of hard cast iron did not penetrate. It fell back after thudding against the hide. And the creature did not so much as turn. While I followed him to the limit of where I dared to go on foot within the range of my oxygen supply, and after I stopped and I saw him marching on, he paid no attention to me. He went over my horizon and out of sight, tirelessly and incomprehensibly, showing, in his every movement, a conscious purpose, but never once, so far as I could see, the slightest sign of consciousness.

20

I WAS WORKING on my tanks and vats. The thing to do was to collect and store the fruit within my fortress and behind my wire as soon as it was ripe. Just how I would process it I did not know. I had tried my 'laboratory' process on specimens of the unripe fruit and sometimes it worked and sometimes it did not. Sometimes I got a sweet-tasting result with the flavour of pineapple and the consistency of dough, and sometimes I got a pullulating mass. But what I thought of, all the time, was of how a creature could have conscious purpose but not the consciousness that went with it. Even ants and bees, if you injured them, became conscious of you and ran away or turned round to attack.

Or was I being too provincial and parochial in my thinking? I ran my electric welding iron slowly down a seam. Because Earth was a crowded planet, with a good supply of oxygen and an infinite variety of species of every order, was it simply that I, born in that environment, could not conceive of a creature that was not competitive and never went to war?

But the thing had looked almost like a man, round-headed, two-legged, two-armed, two-eyed. Did not that imply a similar line of development to that which had produced humanity on Earth? Or, if not humanity, then at least, say, squirrels or kangaroos or apes, or any other of the creatures which on Earth had learned to walk on two legs and to use two others for the purpose of transferring food from earth to mouth? Did the very existence of the thing imply that at one time one part of Mars at least had been covered by trees and forests, while the actions of the thing implied that at least there had been intelligence, once?

I looked at the plain around me, desolate and empty as it was, though at that time it was in fact producing the utmost phase of food and life the planet ever knew. I think it was that, the sight of the plain of which by now I knew every fold and stone in my vicinity, which convinced me. Mars had been like that for such countless ages that whatever preceded it was irrelevant. It was not the creature that was strange but I who was jumping to conclusions.

I looked away to the south, where, beyond a region of utter desert, the southern polar cap must be collecting the moisture from the air, laying it down in layer on layer of frost, ready to release it again in six months' time, after the elapse of a quarter of the Martian year. I had decided already that whatever mobile life there was on Mars, at this stage of the planet's development, regardless of what had gone before, must be capable of crossing that desert, of starting again in the south when the new spring came. The creatures, I had thought, must be highly mobile and large in size. But I had not thought of their subjective characteristics, of their 'character' as it were.

It could not be intelligence that would send them on that twice-annual trek. A creature developing intelligence in that environment would perish before the intelligence, needed to understand the nature of seasonal change, was sufficient to send it out across hundreds of miles of desert in the hope of meeting a new birth of life half across a world. Only instinct, the race-learning that developed from one generation to the next, could be enough to start the process.

Suddenly I felt lonely, more lonely than I had since I had ever comprehended that there were other creatures beside myself upon the planet. I looked around me and the horizon seemed narrower and more pinched, the sky a more ghastly green, and the land more barren. For I understood that I had been wrong to impute either human or animal intelligence to the creatures. I had been wrong to think in terms of backbones and brains. I would have been nearer if I had thought in terms of ostriches and emus and two-legged birds that lived flightlessly their running, instinctive lives on the plains of Earth. I would have been nearer still if I had not thought of the vertebrates at all but of insects and spineless creatures, even more blind and incapable of learning, which only appeared to have intelligence and conscious purpose, and which, because of their intractability, made small boys hate them.

I looked at my bow, which, despite its proved uselessness, still lay near me as I worked. I knew now why I had attempted to shoot the Thing. It had been the natural and inevitable reaction of any human creature to a being whose nature he could not understand and whose mental processes, if any, he could not envisage. It had not only been a senseless will to power. It was something deeper, an atavistic fear.

On Earth, there must have been a time when the intelligent creatures, those capable of curiosity, learning, and some dim self-consciousness, had been at the mercy of the non-intelligent. It might be possible to trace that time back to the contest between the animals and the reptiles, or even farther, to the conflict between the vertebrates and the invertebrates. Man's ancestors then had known fear, and I knew the fear again: the fear of the creatures that were coming to me across the plains of Mars. For human life was intelligent life and its satisfactions were those of conscious appreciation. It was something not understandable, not estimable to me, what blind joys and pleasures creatures however vast could have whose actions were compulsions, who never knew the slightest choice, and whose virtue was their endurance, their ability to sustain purpose and action blindly.

The prospect of sharing a planet with such Things left my mind in a bitter daze. It was as though I were contemplating not the specific difficulties of my lot, my continued uncertainty about my food supply and my knowledge that I would have to fight for it, but something greater. I was contemplating, even as I shrugged my shoulders and went back to work, the nature of life itself, the knowledge that it was at once universal and by no means confined to what we would regard as intelligence. If life were blind, and could exist blindly, through countless generations on a planet, and if human intelligence such as I had were simply a joke or an accident in the universe, then what *was* the use of anything? What was the purpose of anything, even if one presumed a God, a creator, who could conceivably have a purpose?

Perhaps I was on the verge of madness when I was living, still in and near the wreck, during the interval between the coming of the first of the Things and the arrival of the horde. It was as though, on Earth, the knowledge that there were other people, never, after all, so very far away, closed the mind to certain questions. One drew comfort from other people's mere existence. But where people did not exist? Where life was vast, apparently purposeful, yet also futile, serving no conceivable purpose except to sustain itself? There was nothing beautiful to me then in the sight of the brighter stars which shone dimly through the green haze that hung above me. I felt, as I waited—and the trouble was that the waiting lasted several days—that I had sunk to that level, during my life on Mars, at which I contemplated the inner heart, the emptiness and vacancy which existed beneath all human and animal experience of a universe which was as blind and hopeless and as purposeless as I myself would become if I allowed myself to be that way.

It was sheer stubbornness that made me complete my work on the storage vats and begin to pick the fruit. It was stubbornness that made me grin to myself and refuse to admit that I was facing death or undue difficulty. After all, I did not know what else might come, beside these Things. I had not met the second species yet. And I refused to admit that my desert was a desert or that creatures, senseless as they might be, could be incapable of yielding to some form of contact. If a natural man was anything, I thought, he was a naturalist.

21

I WAS PICKING the fruit when it happened. It was ripe so far as I could see, having turned a reddish gold which gave the whole plain a sheen, and I could not understand what held the creatures back. Sensibly, while they did hang back, I worked at my farthest from the wreck. I went out more than a mile to the northwards, picked the melon-like harvest, and put them in sacks which I hung from my tricycle, which I then pushed back to the circumference of my wire. Arriving at the wire, I looked around the horizon, lifted a certain stone, and pulled a hidden switch. With the current disconnected, I entered my compound after disconnecting a portion of the wire, unpacked my cargo and emptied it into the storage vat. Usually I needed, at that point, to go inside the wreck. I would examine my machines and pressure gauges, refill my oxygen cylinder, and note and record the progress of my latest micro-biological experiments with the fruit. I had solved the problem of making it barely edible, and, I hoped, of storing the products, in a dried and dehydrated form. But what the food value was, I could not guess. I was trying, by every means I knew, to grow a variety of yeasts and cultures in the juices, in the hope of producing protein, carbohydrates, and also vitamins.

After spending perhaps half an hour attending to my various chores and researches, I would let myself out of the wreck again, by the simplified and improved airlock I had made by then, take a glance at my vast but still almost empty bins, and set out once more across the plain, working the northward section first.

It was at the end of one of these runs, when I had ridden out on my tricycle and was prepared to pick, that I saw them coming. They were visible to the north of me, a long line of perhaps two dozen heads, picking like locusts so that the horizon behind them looked strangely pale and green, denuded.

I froze where I was. So slow was their progress that I was able to stay and watch them for half an hour. They stopped at intervals. As to what they did with the fruit when they had picked it, I could only make out that they seemed to eat it. I watched, amazed and startled at their apparent digestive process. They themselves looked gross and ripe, well-fed, as well they might if they had grazed, in that fashion, all the way down from the northern pole. Then, hastily, I began to pick what fruit I could. I realised that I would have time to take at least one more load back home. I worked with the speed of despair, went back and retired temporarily behind my wire.

It was mid-morning. I could not expect the night to

intervene. I came out from my wire again with a portable apparatus I had made. It consisted of a battery and a coil of wire and stakes, together with a machine that I can only describe as a mechanical cross-bow. I advanced towards the creatures, unslung my coil, and began to drive in the stakes across their front.

I had judged the speed of their approach carefully to give myself plenty of time to get set up. The wire—the most I had—extended for a hundred yards. Connected to a trembler coil and the battery, it formed a barrier. Behind it, I established myself. I mounted the cross-bow on the tricycle, fitted an arrow in the slot, and wound back the gear which drew back the wire. When I touched the trigger this time, the arrow would be driven with the power, if not the speed, of a rifle bullet.

I must admit that the reason that the apparatus was mounted on the tricycle was that if it did not work, if it could not stop them, then I would have the speed to make my getaway. I had been so unsuccessful against the one creature that I doubted my ability against a dozen, even with the improved apparatus that I had. And I still could not believe that they would not have sufficient intelligence to try to turn my flanks.

They came on, paying no attention to me at all. There was something inexorable about their progress across the plain. I waited for them with mixed feelings. At first, I thought the longer they took the better. I had no wish to try conclusions with them. But the waiting was nerve-racking. After ten minutes my one thought was the wish that they would come and that I could get the experiment over with.

Except for the one on the extreme right, they looked different from the earlier example of their species I had seen. They looked shorter and fatter, and more like perambulating barrels or grease tubs than anything I could conceive. I imagined, wrongly I later believed, that I was facing a tribe or pack of them, with one male and—perhaps, I did not know—a following of females. I could not even dream whether the bi-sexual system was also the rule on Mars.

What destroyed my project was that the 'male' broke from the pack. I watched him with horror and fascination. He came upon a place where I had been cutting fruit. It was an episode which taught me much about his degree of intelligence. I had noticed already that he was going from one to another of the fruit he had severed several days before, and, at every mark he had made on the ground, he altered course slightly and the group altered with him. Now he came to a spot where his tracks were overlaid by mine and the fruit was gone.

He stopped. He looked around the horizon. He showed evidence of distress by moving back and forth across his front while the rest of the line stood waiting. I gasped when I saw what was happening. It was as though he had had a fixed plan in his mind, an area which had to be covered that day, and now that plan had gone awry. But did not that imply intelligence of a sort? Had I not been wrong in my estimates then? I watched him carefully and with anxiety. And then I saw him do what insects do when they are disturbed in their instinctive processes.

While the line stood stopped, he went off alone. He started on my right and he went farther to my right. He began to cut the fruit and mark the ground again, as he had done a few days earlier.

And he was going round my wire. That would not do. I started forward. At least I knew now which one I had to stop. I in turn made a sortie as though in an armoured car. It would have been ludicrous, if it had not been deadly, this conflict between an Earth man with improvised resources and a Martian who had not the *kind* of intelligence which could tell him what was happening.

I approached and fired, still moving forward, at a distance of fifty yards. My cross-bow was capable of sighting like a rifle and I could not miss. I watched the arrow fly, and immediately drew back, half-turning, but watching him, and ready to take to flight.

The arrow penetrated. I think it would have gone through a thin sheet of armoured steel. I saw him stagger. And then, blindly oblivious, he went on.

He went on, as he had been doing, still cutting fruit and marking the ground, in the direction of the wreck! I left my wire fence, which already was outflanked, and rode parallel with him, at a distance of almost a hundred yards, towards the other fence, the one round the wreck, which I had left alive. I was there, watching him, when, reeling and staggering, but apparently understanding nothing, not even his own approaching end, he reached it. I saw him actually touch and breast the wire. I saw the flash.

And he still went on. He fell to earth not more than a few yards from the wreck itself. He tried to get up, and he collapsed again. The rest of the creatures, in line, stood waiting.

I felt simultaneous triumph and dismay. I had killed. I had won a round. And yet my fencing was not strong enough or powerful enough to stop the Things. I saw what happened when the leader died. Indeed, I could only tell when he died by what happened.

The next to him in the line moved forward. He followed the new track of severed fruit and marked ground that the dead leader had made. And the rest of the line moved forward too, as though nothing had happened. They began to 'graze' once more, and they came up against my isolated stretch of wire.

I saw another flash, and one of them convulsed and fell. But neither he nor any other of them paid the slightest attention to that fact. He got up and came on. They went through the wire and advanced towards me. I retreated before them. I fitted another arrow to my bow and fired. I killed again. Riding round and round them, while they remained oblivious to me, I killed four times. Then I had no more arrows left and they kept on, closing their ranks and still razing the crop all around the wreck. At the wreck itself, they split and flowed round it like a tide.

In despair, I looked to the horizon to the northwards. There was so much of the plain that was still untouched. Then I saw, on the horizon to the northwards, the heads and bodies of other groups of Things.

I knew I was defeated. The plain was becoming utter desert round me, and I could not stop the forward movement of the flood.

I took refuge in a sandy, salty patch of earth where no plants grew. I watched the creatures, all that afternoon, eat up my crop. They avoided the salty, sandy area, and at nightfall they were all to the southward, silent, and, I presumed, sleeping.

I went back slowly to the wreck across the utter desert. I looked in my bin, which was undisturbed. I had two layers of fruit, far too little in bulk to last me through the Martian double year. And I had five carcasses in all, gross bulbous things, the dead, insect-minded creatures that I hated.

I shuddered as I went inside. I thought that I would probably have to try to eat the things, but I was already feeling sick, and the thought was worse. I would not have touched or approached any of them except that the first had died almost outside my door.

Then, passing him in the evening light, I saw that a form of decay had set in already. The gross, twisted body was covered with a mauve sheen, presumably of bacteria, and, loathesomely, his extremities were already encrusted with a white powder.

A powder resembling that of the sandy, salty patches in the soil of which I had found only two in all my wanderings. I looked down at the white powder which, raised by my passage, had harmlessly coated me, and felt a sudden disgust of insane proportions. I did not understand Mars. More than not understanding. I suddenly felt frightened of it, madly, to a degree which left my own new certainty of ultimate starvation as little more than a minor, distant, and peaceful threat.

22

I DID NOT expect to sleep that night: I was too near the utter humiliation of despair. I had seen all my work come to nothing and all my hopes vanquished in an afternoon. But that was not the worst of it. What humiliated me beyond bearing was that I had made scarcely a ripple in the life of the plains of Mars. I did not know how it could have been. I had read enough books in my time, fanciful stories of how strange, Earth-men, strangers on strange planets, had mastered their environment by a few quick moves and ruled triumphantly and all-powerfully. Perhaps I had dreamed of something of that sort for myself. But, instead, I found that my situation was more like that of the first white men to penetrate into the great plains of North America: in a strange land and facing strange threats, and always on the brink of starvation, it was, or had been, touch and go whether I would learn enough of what I faced in time or whether I would perish just because I did not realise enough the strangeness.

My camp in the wreck, which had come to seem my home, familiar, and offering security by its permanence, now seemed to me once more what it had been in the first place, a precarious foothold on a world in which the only thing I could expect was the unexpected. Only while, before, I had been ready for anything, including almost any subversion of the laws of nature, I now understood that the natural laws of science must and did apply but that what I lacked was the knowledge, the imagination even, to understand the ways, different from those on Earth, that they could apply.

Bitterly, helplessly, foolishly and ridiculously, I went inside the rocket. I closed the airlock behind me, and in the metal room that was of Earth, that had been built on Earth, and yet which, symbolically it now seemed to me, lay tilted, broken, and useless for its intended purpose, I sat down and put my head between my hands.

I waited, numbly, thinking of nothing, while outside the mild damp evening settled down, the summer damp, the short-lived, beneficent season of growth on Mars. Creatures, I thought, that performed purposeful actions yet were incapable of learning. That was the mistake I had made—it came to me slowly, seeping into my empty mind: I had presumed that, as among the competitive life of Earth, all living creatures could learn and reason, or at least react to the stimulus of pain and death. But the creatures that had swept my plain clear as a cloud of locusts had behaved like locusts. That one should die or suffer when he reached a certain spot had in no way prevented him or any other of them from pressing on. As much might I have thought to teach grass that because it was grazed to the earth in a certain place it should not grow in that place again.

Outside, I knew, the air was mild, with dew soaking into the parched earth. The plants would recover from the loss of their fruit, would grow fresh roots and re-establish themselves to withstand the long drought that lay ahead. Before the next active season came they would fruit again. But by then I would be dead and the shell in which I lived would become an empty sepulchre, a rustless monument to my futility, a warning to some future generation of Earth-men when they came.

I must write a diary, I thought. I must leave a message, which would persist changelessly in the changeless air. Here, I would say, or somewhere in this vicinity, would be found the skeleton of the man who had not understood that peaceful nomadic creatures living in a non-competitive world, would not develop Earth reactions, and would be, because of their very innocence, unstoppable, while their 'minds' if they had any remained incomprehensible to me.

I touched the depths of despair during that evening when I sat in the wreck on Mars. It was not so much the thought of death that embittered me. Everyone must die, and he who is in despair because of that had better not live at all, since whether it is foreseen in six months, six years, or sixty, it is the same. It was my defeat that rankled, the knowledge that I had had success within my grasp and had failed simply because I had not been efficient enough to compete with other, dim-witted creatures for the fruits of an empty plain.

I began to feel angry with myself because I had not gathered in the fruits earlier, even if they were unripe. I felt angry because I had not made larger, stouter fences, with a hundrd thousand volts upon them, so that the spark would leap out and kill whatever approached before it actually touched and broke the wire. My anger touched itself off in me like a spark. It was like a powder train, as though I had been only waiting to explode.

I got up and put on my mask and cylinder, to go outside. I do not know what I hoped to do there. It was night by then, and I had the sense to take my torch, but I cannot dream that I hoped to accomplish anything in the vacancy of the plain beneath the Martian moons. I think, looking back on it, that I must have felt already, unknown to my conscious mind, the faintest vibration of the earth. I must have thought that there was Something out there, and, angry as I was, the existence of anything, if it were only alive and within my reach, was enough to send me out. I had learned one lesson not with my mind but with my soul: that whatever was coming to me I must go out to meet it, for if I waited for it to come to me I would be defeated.

I let myself through the airlock. It was cold and damp outside, and, for the first time since I had been on Mars I believed I could feel a cool wind stirring. The temperature must have been near to freezing, and yet it was not frost but dew that silvered the world around me in the cold hard light of the two small moons. Night on Mars. Incomprehensibly, inexplicably, my anger and despair hardened into an exultation. I walked away quickly from the wreck and went to that little rocky rise of land to which I had first gone when I had been the first man to set foot on the soil of Mars. It was not my dominion, that place. Indeed, in it, I was more helpless than the senseless beasts. But I was the first to try myself in it, and to learn the hard way, and the very stimulus of the cold told me that I was not defeated yet.

I went up on to the little rocky rise and looked all around. I stilled and tensed as soon as my eye caught a glint, a flash.

It was from the south-westward, from the region to which the Things had gone. I saw it again, like searchlights or ships' lights far out at sea. And, beneath me, I felt a rumbling in the ground. It was as though, in the far distance, the sound not carrying through the thin rare air, a shunting engine were running on iron rails.

I remembered the beast I had seen on that other night, the second species, of which I had only seen the light. If it were a beast, I thought. The resemblance came to me again between the greater thing, which illuminated the area of its passage, and some vehicle back on Earth. My mind, stimulated as it was, ran wild with fantastic guesses. Some vehicle manned by an intelligent race perhaps? What, after all, did I know of Mars? It had been too glibly supposed that a space-traveller, landing on a strange planet, would rapidly make contact with the dominant species there. On Earth, if he landed, he would most likely first see cows in the field where his machine touched down. . . . And at nightfall, headlamps along a road. . . .

I was ready for anything when I saw the lights turn in my direction. I remained where I was as they came to me with inconceivable rapidity on a winding course. A vehicle, I thought, it must be. . . . And then again I felt the thunder as of great legs stamping.

I would not abandon my guess at once. Was it not possible that on Mars a civilisation existed that had never known a wheel? But, as the creature came, whatever it was, my mind began to work at lightning speed. No, it was not possible that any civilisation involving mechanical contrivances should exist if there were no wheels. And yet, what could it be, on Mars, that moved at a speed like that? I had already thought enough of the economics, the bio-economics of life in a rarefied atmosphere. How much air must a creature of that size breathe—it seemed to me that even in the Martian gravitational field it must weigh many tons—merely to sustain its body heat? I had begun those speculations when I had first seen the ant-like insects and discovered that they had lungs. Recently, I had seen the great two-legged creatures, but they, though big, had been steady and inexorable rather than active in their movements, and I had not been slow to guess how much of those bloated bodies was used for breathing air. Yet this—

In the bright moonlight, it turned, momentarily, broadside on to me. I saw pale lights along its side that were too like those phosphorescent orbs of deep sea fish for the comparison to escape me. But the thing was a hundred feet in length! And it turned, swiftly and thunderously, and came on towards me!

I stood in startled fright and was ready to run at last. Anger and the exultation of the night were one thing, but when panic came it was black. If I had known which way to run, I would have done so. But the creature—I rejected the vehicle hypothesis now—turned aside when a hundred yards away and passed beneath me. It went on, past me, towards the wreck. . . .

I felt, as it passed, a wave of heat. It was a surge of hot air coming up to me. I could not credit what the thing was, or how it lived, but I knew, suddenly, why it lived and moved at night.

I had not time to think. In the silver light, and with its lights brilliantly illuminating its every movement, I saw it go to the wreck and past it. Was it my imagination that it paused an instant by the wreck, and was it chance that it bathed the rocket for a moment with its light? But it went on. It went to where the man-like creatures lay that I had killed in a scattered group to the northward of the wreck, and there it stopped.

I watched it, fascinated, horrified, and appalled. I was beyond fear and understanding while I watched. For a moment I think I exceeded myself. The strangeness of what I saw was such as to hold my attention and my whole mind so that I even forgot, for instance, the possibilities of what was to happen to myself.

For the creature—if creature it could be called—went to one and then another of the corpses. It seemed to me to inspect them, as though wondering how and why they died. It was a while before I heard a ghastly crunching sound and realised that what was taking place was a gigantic meal.

Watching, fearful beyond panic from my knoll, I tried to understand. This, then, was presumably the Martian Tyrannosaurus. But if I could have understood how any creature, in an almost oxygen-free air, could hope to digest and burn such vast quantities of food, I might have believed it better. As it was, I began numbly to think of myself again, of how those creatures, whatever they were, were all that had been left to me of my harvest. What I was seeing now, applied to myself, was the taking away from him who had not even that which he had. My anger came again in such insane proportions that if I had had the means to attack I would have done so, though the creature proved to be the legendary fire-breathing dragon itself.

But I saw it stop, and turn in the moonlight, and face the wreck again. I saw its lights, its radiance rather, that it cast before it, bathe the broken rocket and all the scene of what had been my home. And I saw that light wink on and off, and change colour, running up and down the visual scale from ultra-violet to infra-red and back.

I think I guessed what was going to happen. I took one pace forward. Then the creature was advancing on the wreck, as though with threatening intent, and I was shouting in my mask and running. If the wreck was damaged—and the creature was big enough to do it—then I was completely lost. It would be better to die then and there in defence of my habitation and my machines.

Neither the sound of my shouting nor my running made any difference to the thing. It advanced upon the wreck with a strange, slow caution, as though, I wildly imagined, it expected the mass of dead steel to get up and retreat from it or attack. I watched with horror, thinking as I ran in the moonlight that that was my end.

I think it was by accident that my torch flicked on. Certainly the moonlight was bright enough for me not to need it, and I never had used it in the open while on Mars.

The great thing turned. I had a vision of a gaping mouth that was not so much a jaw as a nightmare opening fringed, as though by a beard, with tiny arms or legs which might be used, I could only guess, as are the similar tentacles of crustaceans, to break up food and to push it in. Then I could see no more. I was bathed with a narrow, brilliant beam of light, of an intensity, it seemed to me, of sunlight.

I went down on my knees. Terror, when it reaches a certain stage, paralyses all the impulses, so that the mind operates seemingly in a vacuum, conscious of nothing but its own existence. Blinded, bowed, I knelt there.

The light flicked on, flicked off. As I had seen it do already, it ran up and down the visual scale. But the creature had stopped. It was not approaching me.

I think it must have been for a minute that I knelt like that. I was conscious only of the changing colours of the light and its intermissions. Somehow—how can I convey this?—I gained from those steady charges, unhurried and unstartling as they were, a sense of peace.

A thought broke through the mask that seemed to have settled on my brain. I put my torch before me and pressed the switch. I pressed it and flicked it off again. It was my final throw of madness, to attempt to communicate with a land-borne deep-sea monster.

It worked! The radiance, the changing colours faded. In its place, after a pause, came a single flashing light, the echo and image of my torch.

I flashed. I used my rudimentary knowledge of the Morse code. The letters came back to me, echoing my spacing, senselessly and meaninglessly, but accurately.

Not understanding, not even daring to imagine what I had discovered, I abandoned my useless groups and phrases. I sent flashes in groups of one and two and three and four. I received an identical answer. Then I sent a group of, counting carefully, ten.

The answer I got was nine.

I paused and waited. I received a signal that seemed to me to be a meaningless jumble. I tried to imitate it, and must have succeeded, for I got another one, more difficult, I failed at that, and we both paused, waiting.

I knew I was faced with a creature of strange and complex intelligence which could not count to ten. What 'she' knew, I can't imagine. That, I imagine, she had discovered some strange and puny, dim-witted creature in her domain.

She backed away and went carefully round me and away into the night. Behind her, where she had lain while she 'talked' with me, the ground glowed brightly.

When day came, that patch of ground was bare and covered with white, like salt. And, though three of the corpses outside the wreck were left, they were pullulating masses, mauve in the centre, deliquescent with a shining liquid, but crusted white on the outside with a powder that seemed to grow like fungus.

Red-eyed, sleeplessly, balefully, I looked at them.

It was by eating such things as that, that the monstrous creatures lived at night—lived on Mars, in that thin atmosphere, supporting an intelligence of some kind, and radiating a body heat which told of a metabolism and power beyond my dreams.

23

I DID NOT understand the full horror at first. At first I simply stood and looked at the barren plain around me, at the stripped land, and wondered if the creatures would come back. Even about that I only wondered if I would survive their return, or whether, if they had gone on to the southward with their ever onward-rolling wave of life, I would be left to starve slowly on the fruitless plain.

It was only slowly as I stood there, staring and trying to recall again and again the incidents of the night, that I began dimly to understand. It was then that horror came.

For they were men, those creatures that had come to me across the plain in daylight, and whom I had killed. It was true that they had defeated me by their stupidity, by their failure to respond to threats, to experience, or even to the fate of the first of them to die. But they were still 'men': two-legged, lung-breathing animals that lived on the fruits of the soil, wandering and nomadic. They were as much 'men' as the Martian 'insect' was an insect, as the 'plants' were plants, and as much as the substance of the desert all around me could be described by our common name of 'earth'.

Only they were not the highest form of creation on Mars. If what I had seen had the significance I thought it had they were the herds, the field creatures, the cattle of a greater creature that preyed on them at night: something biologically inconceivable to us—and this was where the horror began—something that on Mars at least, could only be conceived of as a higher form.

Physically shattered by the night, I stood swaying by the wreck under a crushing mental blow. It was minutes, hours maybe, before I began to know what it was. And then my grasp of it, of the reason why I was so appalled, came only slowly to me, item by item, as I thought. For I was facing an experience that had never come to a human being before.

Man might have thought that, venturing on other planets, he would face new experiences. But he had not. He had thought that he would face the same experiences as on Earth, but of a different order. Perhaps it had been impossible for him to imagine anything quite new, for which his experience had not prepared him. But I, unmoving, not daring to examine the corpses nor the remains of the midnight feast, and yet fascinated, unable to go away and rest and leave the scene, had slowly to understand the significance of what had happened before my eyes.

My mind moved darkly, as though in prayer. Why had man ever wished to venture from his world? Why had I come? Why had common people everywhere been interested, passionately interested, in space-flight, as soon as its possibility began to tentatively to be established? The need, the urge, was rooted in the human situation, in what every man knew of the universe and of his own position in it. He had had a hope, a strange hope. But on that morning on Mars that hope in me was quelled and my soul seemed to shrivel, my emotions freeze.

Man found himself. He was a speck of life on that cooling planet, Earth, amid myriads of his fellows. He became aware that the universe around him was incomprehensible in its vastness. He became aware that time, as he knew it, was hardly an instant in the ages that had been and which must be to come. He knew, too soon he knew, that he personally was condemned to die.

But he also knew that, around him on the Earth, were countless other creatures, which he could dominate. He ruled his planet, and he, alone of the creatures on it, had had the mind, the intelligence, to lift his eyes, his spirit, his comprehension to the stars. Space might be infinite, but he alone had dreamed of crossing it. Time might be infinite, but he had dreamed that his race, his descendants might go on, as the masters they were, to spread explosively through the universe, and to populate it, so that they were no longer dependent on the fate of any one planet. And, in the end, the spirit of man, that highest creature of creation, who had taken his fate into his own hands and become, in a large sense, self-created, would comprehend it all. He would understand eternity, and by so doing become the master of it. Because the other thing, to be a mite only, to be only a crawling thing that lived for a while on the body of a dying world, as dependent on his environment as the bacteria that thrived for a while in the body of a larger creature, and so to end in nothingness, was too terrible to contemplate.

Perhaps that was why I, even I, had left my home, had played fretfully with one thing and another, with various ways of living, until my chance had come to carry human experience just one stage further, to be a part of the first expedition to leave the Earth, though I had not thought of it before. Not until that morning after the night on Mars. Not until it began to penetrate to me, however dimly, that the ecology of the planet was not that of Earth: that men were not necessarily the Lords of Creation in a biological sense at all, but only a stage in the development of life, something that on Earth might have its flower just as, in our past, the invertebrates, the reptiles, had had theirs, but which—it was a hypothesis only in those first instants, but a dreadful one—had passed that stage on Mars.

As I stared at those corpses with red-rimmed eyes on that

first morning of knowledge on the planet Mars, I did not understand it all. I did not think in evolutionary terms, nor is it possible for me now to separate my actual thoughts at that time from the accretions that came later, during the following weeks, when I faced the problem constantly, night and day. What I actually thought, and what I am quite sure must have first come to me in that awakening, if only as a bare idea, for it was basic to my understanding, was that great glimpse of the obvious to which my whole experience of Mars had been working up, and, unknown to myself, preparing me.

My mind went back over the preceding weeks, from and to the moment when I had first brought the rocket in to land and tumbled out on to the Martian surface. I had found life, but had been puzzled to find only a single type of plant. I had found insects, but only a single, highly developed, form. It had been as though, on an older world than Earth, a sheering process had been at work; as though out of the proliferation of such varied species as we knew, only the best of each order, the most highly adapted, had been able to survive. And then I had found a representative of the animal kingdom. Had it been a surprise that these should prove to be a gross and unintelligent, degenerate race of men? I had thought already that, in that thin air, all animal creatures would have to be all lung, and it would be impossible, in the conditions existing on the planet, for any creature to retain that fine adjustment of temperature, pressure, and chemical nicety that was necessary to maintain a finely adjusted nervous system.

Only what I had not thought of was that there might be some other creature which had developed since Mars was filled with life like Earth. That such a creature should come into being during the slow decline of the planet's life was perhaps inevitable, but I had not thought of it any more than I had solved the problem of how life had come into being at all on a planet that now possessed no sort of sea and which lacked what life most needed, oxygen and water.

Such a creature would have to be independent of supplies of oxygen from the air. It would have to be able to sustain its body heat regardless of heat or cold or night. It would have to derive its total energy from lower forms of life. It, on Mars, would have to prey on the animal kingdom, and be dependent on it, even as animals on Earth lived only because of the plants that drew energy from the sunlight and the bacteria that drew nitrogen from the air and made it available in the soil. On Earth, man drew oxygen from the air and drank water as a mineral, but for all the rest he was completely dependent on the complex substances built up by other living things. Only one stage further would evolution have to go, and then . . .

I stared with horror at those decaying masses which I was responsible for having killed so near the wreck. That mauve fluid--could it be the blood? The lung substance, oxygenated, as red human blood was, containing and carrying out to the living tissues not only nourishment, the fuel, but the burning agent too, the whole chemical apparatus for release of power? And what of the white crystalline powder that was slowly encrusting the mass as it decayed? A fungus? Or a virus? Or bacteria? Something, I imagined, that seized on the rare elements, the ones that were rarest and most needed on the planet Mars. Something that seized hydroxides, that retained the substance of life as yeasts and fungi did on Earth.

What I was looking at was a field of life which a higher creature had exploited; a creature which, I was sure now, had no lungs, and drew in no substances in unprocessed form; a Thing which had no need to exist on Earth, where oxygen was still plentiful in our atmosphere, and water could be had almost anywhere; a Thing which, uninhibited by the need to restrict its size, as it would on our heavier planet, found the animal kingdom its natural prey, though animals were represented on Mars only by a crude caricature of the race of men.

Cannibals, I thought. Crusoe's island, so quiet and peaceful-seeming, had had its other side, the side of bestiality, of savagery, and his instinct had been to kill, and kill, and kill, because he, with his preconceptions about God and the human place in the universe, was outraged.

Only Crusoe had not dared to kill. He had not dared, even with his guns, to take on a whole alien world in mortal combat. Instead, he had had to come to terms with what he found, accept the fact of his own weakness, and flee and hide like a hunted thing, and meanwhile try to live.

He who had herds and crops and air and water.

24

I LOOKED at the piles of crystals that had been corpses. I walked around them warily. I tried to remember if the creature had consumed those bodies which were freshest or those in which the decay had been most advanced. Grimly, and as though in confirmation of my horror, I thought that it had been those which were most decayed.

I hesitated to touch the crystals. On Earth the instruments of decay were species of bacteria. I had never heard of a bacteria producing crystals. But a virus might. A virus might be crystals. There were types of virus on Earth that could be crystallised out, and then, when put in contact with their food, they became as virulent as before.

I took no chances. I went back to the wreck and made myself a scoop. I brought out lenses from the telescopes, and glass jars with screw tops, and a jug of water.

What did I think I was going to do? Did I think that I, with no knowledge of biochemistry, and with such crude equipment, was going to embark on a fractional analysis, and so discover the secret of higher life on Mars? I can only say what I did.

I looked at the crystals, after I had separated a few of them, beneath my most powerful lenses. I noticed that they were long, needle-shaped structures, with pyramidal points. Seen against the light, and singly, they were translucent and had a tinge of blue. I contemplated them for some time as though mere staring would yield up to me a secret of the universe.

Then I looked around me. I saw, still barely perceptible on that unchanging surface and in that still air, the white trail where the monster had rested. I rose to my feet suddenly and went across to it. With infinite care, I scraped off a sample of the white amorphous powder of which the trail was composed.

Restlessly, I looked at it beneath my glass. The inspection was fruitless. No structure at all was apparent in the powder. It was only apparent that, despite my care, I had picked up specks of dust and earth among the white. It was with the idea of obtaining a pure sample that I dissolved the powder in a little water. By solution and evaporation. . . .

I stopped in the middle of my experiment. I picked up the jar of fluid and held it in my hand. Was it my imagination it was warm? I went quickly for a thermometer.

Not only did the white powder produce heat when mixed with water but when it had been dissolved, and the water evaporated off again, it was no longer an amorphous powder. It became long, needle-shaped crystals with pyramidal ends. . . .

I thought I had the answer to the problem in my grasp, but then I noticed that the crystals formed from the powder lacked one thing that the others had: the tinge of blue. I knew enough to suppose some fine and subtle difference of molecular structure between the two.

I remained, squatting in the desert with the powder and the two sorts of crystals before me, for quite an hour. But my mind was not idle. I thought in terms of creatures that maybe had no lungs, that drew their nourishment from one source, and digested it in one stomach, and, maybe by another digestive system, imbibed an oxygenating agent. Water and air. . . . On a planet like Earth those thing were to be had freely from the environment, but on an arid planet any creature which was to be independent of its environment would need another, more subtle source.

My mind played not so much with ideas as on them, like the swift visions revealed by summer lightning. I thought of carbon and saltpetre, of gunpowder and explosives, man-made from oxygenising agents. I thought of sources of power within that carbon-oxygen-hydrogen cycle that contained all life.

I got up abruptly. I felt at the same time an elevation of the spirit and an obsession. It was something resulting out of my grim patience and determination. It was something I had never known in my life before, the sensation of seeing a thing round and seeing it whole.

Even my actions were not entirely sane for one who was working on a wild hypothesis. I went to the wreck with impatience and decision, as though I knew exactly what I was going for. I went into the wrecked compartment of the stern and my glance played on the old charging plant which had supplied the ship with electric power but which I had never used. I looked at the great fuel tank beside it. There was plenty of fuel, but I had had no air to burn it in, no oxygen to spare. Quickly, I drew off a quantity of fuel into a jar and brought it out with me, trailing also a coil of wire.

I sat for a moment in the desert, away from the wreck with the jar of petroleum fuel open before me and a scoopful of crystals in my hand. Recklessly, I dropped them in. The fuel took on a bright mauve tinge! I waited for something to happen, but nothing did.

To the two ends of my wire I attached an inch of fuse wire. I dropped it into the solution and forced on the lid over the wire. I went back to the wreck then, paying out wire as I went. On the other end of the wire was a plug for connection to the battery power supply. I hesitated for a moment, looked back across the desert, then plunged the plug into its socket.

I even had the sense to throw myself down as I did so, which was just as well, for, as the fuse wire flashed the explosion occurred with a thunderous roar.

It was moments before chunks of earth and rock had stopped falling about me and clattering against the metal of the wreck, and only then could I arise and view, with sombre satisfaction, the smoking crater in the desert.

I gave up being a materialist in that moment. I no longer speculated on the nature of humanity, on man's smallness, his short span of life, and the fact that, to some higher creature, he might be as grass. Instead, I returned to my faith in the organising power of the human brain, its ability to organise a universe around it: if need be within its life-span.

25

WHEN I WAS ready to go, I was not in any hurry. I had made my preparations meticulously, but even so to leave the rocket which had been my home, and my mine of all material, and to chance myself on the distant Martian surface, as I would have to do to overtake the wave of life, with all the unknown dangers and contests that that involved, was not a thing for haste.

I looked at my machine, my half-track. Perhaps still, to anyone who did not know its origin, it must look crude and improvised, the result of a castaway's labour with rough tools. But to me, aware of its engineering soundness, it was as different from what my tricycle had been as a boat must have been to Crusoe compared with his improvised life-rafts of lashed-up spars.

There was little left in the wreck but an empty shell. Even some of the plates had been incorporated in my vehicle, welded there with the ample power I had had ever since; with extreme care, and modification of the carburettor, I had made the charging plant work on the fuel-crystal mixture. Now the charging plant itself was incorporated in the vehicle, as a prime mover and a source of power.

That I still rode on and not in the thing had been a matter of choice. I had been limited only by the weight which could be supported by the wheels and tracks in the light gravitational field of Mars. But I had favoured the shape and nature of an open truck. Balance and a low centre of gravity had been important, for though the gravitational field was low the mass of my equipment remained the same: any tall vehicle on Mars would soon turn over at the slightest bend or corner.

I prowled around the wreck, seeking anything more that could conceivably be of use to me as spares. Then I went to the truck and inspected its items one by one for a final check.

Slung between the axles were the bins which I had made to contain the fruit when I had thought of myself as an agriculturalist and not a hunter. Now they were topped to the limit with fuel, sealed down, in which was dissolved my total supply of crystals. Those bins were padded, so far as possible, against the jolting of the machine. I was no more happy than need be about the stability of the mixture.

Forward of the bins was my air and water plant, powered by electricity now and comprising chiefly a motor-driven pump. As part of my final check I ran the motor up. At three thousand revs the pump came into action. I watched the thermometers and pressure gauges. The water came off first and there was a long pause before I began to get the liquid air, but it came in the end. After checking the pressure and the fact that the air tank was already full I stopped that motor.

Above the bins, on trays beneath an awning, I kept my food supply. Pitifully small it looked. That was the grim reason I was going, into the unknown.

The driving seat was a bench above the battery. The steering was mechanical and none too good, though I expected to use the machine on long straight courses. The controls were electric, and no more than resistances and switches to the motors. Already on the seat, like a dummy human being, was the pressure suit I would wear at night, while a mask was connected to the air supply and ready.

I walked round to the back of the truck and looked at the equipment there. I had taken everything, everything I could conceive of being useful. It made a tall, broad load. If I struck loose sand or rough terrain much of it might have to be dumped.

I looked back at the wreck. I had hoped to live there, pursuing peaceful agriculture and building slowly. It was not my fault that I had not been able to live like that on Mars. I felt a certain bitterness on seeing all that steel, and all those closed compartments. Even then, to stay there looked the safer way to live. Despite all my preparations, and all the equipment I carried with me, I was aware of the chance that I might break down, that I might find myself lacking something that could only be found within the wreck.

But it was already almost noon, and I climbed on board. I took off the mask I was wearing and slipped on the other, that was attached to the machine. I put my portable oxygen cylinder into the rack I had made for it, where it would be instantly accessible beside me and connected it to the liquid oxygen tank for charging.

I closed the switch that started the charging motor. I let it run for a moment then looked at the voltage dial. Tentatively, I pulled the motor switch, then seized the steering bar as the vehicle lurched into motion.

I did not look back at the wreck. It would have been as futile as to look up into the sky in search of the planet Earth. Instead, after circling half round my old works and rubbish, I set course due south across the plain of Mars.

Somewhere in that direction, and still moving away from me at fifteen miles a day, was the wave of Martian life. The days and weeks had passed since the creatures had come to me. I would have to go to the equator and beyond.

But that was the way life was lived on the arid planet. A man does not adapt his environment to suit himself until he has first adapted himself to his local world.

Later, I would come back, but not until I had tried conclusions once again with those creatures that were physiologically my superiors. On the front of my machine, in a carefully sprung support, was my single powerful light bulb. I tested it as I rode, then switched it off again. I could not take risks with burning the filament out, for though I could make vehicles, pumps, and instruments, I had not, for all my ingenuity, been able to make another light bulb. I even went off, knowing I had been defeated in my attempts to construct an article that could be bought in any cut-price store on Earth.

26

ENCLOSED IN ITS narrow horizons, and under that Martian sky, which was sometimes clear and almost black, and flecked with stars at noonday, and sometimes vague and vaporous, with a green-blue tinge, the plain was grey and endless. I covered fifty miles that first day, and seventy-five the second, and all the time the vegetation, such as it was, grew sparser.

By the third day, I was glad if I saw a shred of green in

fifty yards. The ground was stony. Once I had to circumnavigate a patch of drifting sand a hundred yards across. It was fine as dust and rose in drifting clouds when I let one wheel stray into it.

The prospect became more grim. I had estimated a fixed rate for the creatures' travel, but, although I was not yet at the equator by my calculations, there seemed little for them to pause for in that endless desolation. It was more likely, I thought, that, having eaten their way from the northern polar regions, and grown sleek and fat, both the man-like creatures and those that fed on them, they would from that point make all speed southward, towards the lush feeding grounds of the southern pole, there to await the spring.

I could follow them even there—provided I did not meet with unexpected difficulties or have to make too great deviations on the way.

I was not sure about that. Mars, seen from Earth, and seen by me during my approach to it, had not an entirely uniform surface. Apart from the climatic colours, which changed with the ripening of the seasons, there were areas of permanent difference. But no one knew of what the difference was composed.

I went with my eyes open, knowing that one good mountain range would stop me. But for the first week I did nothing but cross that endless plain.

I would rise stiff and cold in the morning. Wearing the pressure suit at night allowed me at least to maintain a pressure in my body at which I could sleep without actually freezing, and it relieved me from the eternal chafing of a face-mask, but with pressure in it the suit was stiff and uncomfortable. I slept for just so long as I was too weary to even try to turn, and in the morning I always put on my face-mask with the portable cylinder first, then moved and exercised to raise my body heat.

I ate before I started. It was too much of a performance to do otherwise. Even 'ate' is something of an exaggeration.

While living in the wreck, I had been able to keep up the temperature and pressure in my living quarters. Now, living in the open all the time, a thing I would not have dreamed possible when first I came to Mars, I craved always for hot drinks. Whatever it was I had for food, a luxury such as tinned meat or a horrid mess resulting from my 'processing' of the Martian fruit, would go into the pot which I heated, as I did everything else, from the battery of my machine. Then, as a kind of stew, I drank it, replacing my mask and breathing between the gulps.

It might be thought that a man could not live for long in that way, but a man can live long in almost any way provided that he has to and his basic needs are met.

Then I drove. I drove in the direction the compass needle pointed, and concentrated on the ground ahead. Every now and then I would look up and see the close horizon exactly as it was before. Sometimes the circle of sky around me would be just faintly irregular. Sometimes, being on the top of a gentle rise, I would be able to see farther than the regular two-and-half miles ahead. A vista of five miles was a view.

At noon I would stop and cook and eat, and again at six. I made camp then, pegging out an awning from the side of my machine. Somehow it gave me comfort to be covered, though I never proved conclusively that I gained any benefit when in my pressure suit. We are creatures of Earth habit, even I. We do not lie in the open for choice, beneath the sky, not even in the deserts of the planet where we live.

The earth turned pale yellow when I was one week out. There was no doubt about the junction. It took the form of a geological fault or rift about three feet high, and beyond it the horizon looked lop-sided.

I stopped for a while on that day. Partly it was the need to ease the machine across the fault, partly because I was puzzled by the change. I wondered why scientists and astronomers on Earth had formed no theories as to the evolution of my planet. Why was Mars flat, with wide patches of faint colour? Why not, in view of its thin atmosphere, mountainous and jagged, like the moon? Doubtless it was a matter of indifference, when viewed from Earth, but to a man striving across the planet it was of great moment. Had the planet once been covered by a sea? And had life risen on it as it had on Earth, slowly, from watery beginnings, to become a competing horde of species, until, by desiccation, only a few, the best survivors, had been left? And at what stage of such a process had the new form come, the night-living independent monsters?

I stopped and thought, rode on, and thought again. Knowledge was what I craved. I looked down at the new ground of yellow sandstone and wondered if I might find fossils.

When I looked up, there was a range of low white hills before me. Though they were rounded and chalk-like, I knew, from the moment I saw them, that I would never get my machine across.

27

I WENT UP the slabs slowly, dragging one foot after the other and pausing every four or five steps to breathe harshly and desperately, bending forward, resting my hands on my knees, and swaying as I stood. As I came to the top of each slab, to the three or four foot step that led up to the next, I waited for minutes until my heart had ceased its turmoil and my pulse was back almost to normal. Then I climbed the step, and often sat there, on the lip, looking down far across the slope to where my machine lay in the plain. Though I had climbed only five hundred feet, and covered a horizontal distance of only twice that amount since I had stopped my engine and set out on foot, I suffered as does an Everest climber on the summit.

My condition had deteriorated during the journey across the plain. Also it was the first attempt at serious climbing I had made or had occasion to make since I arrived on Mars. I had acclimatised, or I had imagined I had acclimatised very well while I had been living on the flat, but the first attempt at prolonged physical effort had found me out. It was not that there was any appreciable fall in pressure after the distance I had covered. It was just that the plain itself was at an atmospheric 'altitude' above that of Everest's summit, and even breathing oxygen it was beyond the limit of human physiology to go on from there.

I turned and looked at the steps before me. How many more were there? I did not know. The slope was convex on the side that I was climbing and its summit was hidden from anyone upon its surface. The slabs would be less steep, that was all, I thought, swaying and looking up. If I had come so far, I must be able to do the rest, even though, judging by the formation and angle of the chalk-white rock, the slope on the *other* side would be precipitous and steep. I began again, toiling upward foot by foot and inch by inch, knowing the futility of it, knowing that I could never get my machine across and that if I descended the other side I would never be able to retrace my steps, but impelled by the final impulse, which had come to me when I had ridden as far as the machine would go and been checked by the first upward step of the outward-sloping slabs: to see, as a final, useless, accomplishment, what lay on the other side.

The deadweight of my oxygen cylinder held me back. I must have been becoming hazy in my mind, for I imagined at one moment that I would only have to cast it aside and I would mount like the great-lunged creatures I had been following, step by easy step, like a flight of stairs. Or like the other creatures, the night-living ones, who were independent of all air and could live on the most barren planet provided only they found the substances they needed. But I did not in fact touch my mask, though there was a pain like a band around my chest and the oxygen was scalding me with its cold as I allowed it to pour into my mask in quantities I had not used before. I suffered excruciatingly from thirst, and my lips were becoming raw. I thought, light-headedly, for a while, that what I was searching for was a spring, a pool of fresh, clean water that would lie somewhere near the summit.

It was: breathe, breathe, breathe, step, breathe, breathe. It had never come to me, on Earth, what the Himalayan mountaineers meant when they said that, at maximum altitude, they were taking six breaths for every step. Now I knew, and I knew too that there was a nagging in my mind. Sooner or later I would have to make the calculation that they made: as to how long the oxygen supply in the cylinder would last, so that I could turn and take the easier way down, and get back to my machine and the source of air before I was left asphyxiating on the heights.

Not yet. I could not plead that excuse for some hours yet. I must go on. I must get to the summit before it happened. But why? Why even see what lay beyond, when I could not follow with my transport? If there were a pass. . . . But this was the pass. It was the lowest slope in all the range of hills, and I had found, on one of the lower steps, a pile of crystals that told its story: some creature, ageing doubtless, and with its last food left now some days behind, had failed to make the slope and died. So I . . .

I did not complete that thought. That was, after all, why I was climbing up the slope: because it was all I could do but sit by my machine and wait and contemplate my end. Far from the wreck, and checked in mid-flight across the plains of Mars, there was nothing for me now. I was continuing, on foot, for the last few yards and vertical feet an experiment that had proved abortive. When I went down again . . . It was the thought of the nothingness that would await me when I went down that forced me on.

I had come too far, too slowly, and too late. There was

nothing for me now but wilderness below that range of hills. Shortly—for already the angle of the steps was easing off—I would see the southern plain of Mars, a plain, I did not doubt, exactly like the northern. And, having seen, I would be left with an empty vision of the promised land.

I stopped again, and sat, resting my hands on the rock and hanging my head between my arms. Perhaps there would be one more stage, or maybe two. My eyes must have been glazed, unfocused as I stared down at the rock. I felt the pain of its brilliance in the sunlight. Dimly I remembered what I had perceived before: that it was neither chalk nor salt, but some limestone probably, smoothed and rounded though it could not be for a million ages that the puny range had been lapped by seas or dissolved by rain on the equator there, on Mars.

As my breath came back, I looked up again, towards the crest. I knew I would not be able to see the horizon, but only the sky beyond it yet, but as I looked, my gaze became fixed and set.

I staggered to my feet, took a few steps farther, staggered again, and flung and leant myself against the final step. I scrambled up on it, and looked, gasping and staring at a new white crest across a gulf.

Not yet was there any glimpse of the southern plain. Instead, a mile from me, rose another range, while in between was a canyon, the steep terraced slopes of which I could see leading up to the other summit in the sunlight, though the bottom was in the shade.

It was final, that was my first thought. I had had, at the back of my mind, some thought of spying out the land, of finding the easiest route, and then, by infinite labour, by wires and pitons and days of labour, getting my machine to the top and over. But now, with the gulf before me, that was quite washed out. Not in months could I get my transport both up and over, and down, and up again. And for all I knew the range might go on, fold after fold, all the way across the arid centre and southern tropic of the planet. The very fact that the range ran east and west, and thus cast no shadow to the rising or setting sun, would make it invisible from Earth. Telescopes looking down on a planet could not see mountains but only shadows cast by them.

I sat on the crest, and it seemed to me that for the first time since I had been on Mars a faint breeze stirred. I felt its movement in my hair as I looked across the gulf before me. I waited, rested, and let the hope drain out of me to acceptance.

Slowly, because there was nothing else to do, I eased myself towards the edge. I wished to look down into the gulf before I turned and went back to my machine and began to trek to east and west in search of a gap in the range that I knew already did not exist.

The edge was sharp and steep where I had happened to reach the summit, and I lay down on my face to look down over.

28

IT WAS a flower, not unlike a rose, with a faint pink tinge. It was growing on a ledge above the terrace I was looking down upon. And when I reached out a hand to touch it, it burst, and showered me with a million fragments of tiny crystals.

I went on looking. I looked at my hand, surprised to find that it contained nothing but was powdered, as though with pollen. Then I looked down at the terrace, where other pastel-coloured flowers and plant fronds grew. I scrambled to my knees and then to my feet, and went to where a rock-fall gave a ready path to the lower level.

The rock-fall had been used, that and half a dozen others. It was as though an army had passed across it. I tried to envisage the passes, the paths and crossings all along the ranges, where the migratory creatures passed twice a year across the barren regions. But chiefly I was interested in those flowers. I had seen a rose, and it had proved to be a complete illusion.

They, the plants and flowers, only lay in cul-de-sacs along the terrace. Where anything had passed, even within a dozen yards, they did not exist. And when I moved towards them along the level they dispersed before me, shattered, it seemed, by the tiniest vibration of my approaching movement. It was only when I moved stealthily, hardly breathing in my mask, that I could come to them.

Plants? They were crystalline and transparent. They were crystal plants such as we used to grow as children, from saturated solutions in a jar of water.

Only there was no water there. They were arid products of a mineral world, and when, driven beyond endurance by the thought of water, I took my water-bottle from my belt and uncorked it, ready to take a drink, they fell in swathes around me.

It was not vibration that killed them, after all, but moisture, even the perspiration from my skin, which was dispersed in the air around me by any sudden movement. And when I noticed that my water-bottle felt sticky and looked at it, I saw that it was not the bottle but my hand, which had been powdered by the brittle substance of the plants by that time. It had gone damp with a viscous mixture, as though it had been covered with powdered sugar on a damp and steamy day on Earth.

For a moment I was in a panic. God knew what I thought. I tried to wipe my hand and half expected to see the crystals begin to grow on it. But nothing of that sort happened. It was only that, as I shook my water-bottle, further swathes of destruction were caused among the mineral plants around me. Hurriedly, I drank, then corked it.

I wondered, too late, whether I had been wise to drink

with so much of the powder in the air and on my person. The water had a sweet taste, unlike anything I had known, and I could not imagine what alien form of life I might have introduced into my body.

For a while, I simply stood, ready for any agony, any pain. I looked down into the shadowed valley below me, beyond the terrace edge. The shadow was going off it now, as the sun came round to the west to shine along it.

I waited so long, that I found I had licked my lips unconsciously. I was aware of it only when I felt a taste of renewed sweetness in my mouth. I think I went mad for a moment then. It was an instant's rage at the inexplicable quality of the phenomenon with which I was confronted. It was an instant's knowledge that, not knowing what I had to fear, I could not do right by taking forethought. It was a momentary willingness to die, to get it over.

I tore the mask from my face and deliberately licked my hand then put the mask back on. I revelled in the sweet-salt taste. I had a momentary sense of triumph. At least I had gained that—a taste of attractive food again—before I died! Then I wondered with horror what I had done.

Again I waited to die, and did not. Instead, I felt a craving. I had not known the panic and terror I was in until I felt the agony of hope. Suppose—just suppose, I told myself—that these things could be eaten. . . . My mind went dark with suppositions. They were mineral creatures, growing in arid air from powdered rock. They could not be living. They must be raw minerals, creations of the breeze and air perhaps. And yet they could not have attained their shapes—their same shapes, for I could identify a dominant species and several more—unless they had had some cause to adopt the form.

Standing on that ledge above the valley, I lived instants of terror and agony, hope, and fear. Pain, had it come, would have been a quick release. But I did not know. I was ready to call on God to tell Him that I did not know, the very God I had thought I hated. For minerals will crystallise out in the same form, again and again, precise to every facet and every angle. Yet minerals cannot duplicate themselves, unless and except that certain viruses are minerals, of a similar basic structure only more complex. Most likely, I thought, it was another drug that I was taking, something infinitely habit-forming, that paralysed the centres of the brain. I remembered my experiment with the 'honey' of the insects.

But I was one who was otherwise condemned to die. I saw my future before me, brutal and short as it would be. I could go back. I could fell these accursed 'plants'. I could mount my machine again and ride off into the desert, there to perish slowly.

I walked to the 'plants' before me. I held out my hands and caught their substance as they dissolved. I took off my mask and ate, and it was like eating treacle or sucking sugar cane. The only thing was, it increased my thirst, and I had to wash the substance down with copious draughts of water.

I did not fall insensible. I can hardly have eaten an ounce or two before I felt as though I had had a meal. I felt comfortably weary, and had it not been that I was becoming concerned about my oxygen supply, and the need to get back to my machine before darkness fell, I would have lain down where I was and rested.

As it was, I took a lazy, yet comparatively energetic step towards the terrace edge. The sunlight was creeping round into the valley now. It was my one opportunity to see what lay below me and make new plans.

The terraces descended in steps to the valley floor on my side as upon the other. They were like gardens, like European vineyards, without a tenant or a master.

But in the bottom of the valley, on a floor of arid rock, lay one of my creatures of the night. She was—how can I describe it?—she was suckling her brood of young.

29

THAT NIGHT I watched the skyline of the hills. Twice in the darkness I saw reflected lights among the peaks. For a while, cautiously, I ran my engine to charge the battery and work the air and water production plant. The air-compresser worked as well as always, but the water was slow in coming. After an hour, I had gained only half a pint. On the other side of the hills the air would be even dryer. That fact might be fatal to me if, as I hoped, I had reached my journey's end.

Then I lay, still awake, still watchful, looking up at the star-filled sky, and considered a form of life that had never been on Earth. On Earth no life could exist that was born of dryness, that dissolved and became something else at a touch of moisture. Even on Mars only a narrow region, a valley sheltered by hills from cloud and moisture, could have been its birthplace, and that near the equator of the planet. Thinking of it, and seeing the inevitability that life would be born in, and adapted to, all conditions, I wondered what form what we knew as life would take on gaseous bodies like the sun, on worlds of snow and ice and frozen gases like the planet Neptune. For what I had seen seemed to imply, to me, that life was not an unique thing, existing only in a form adapted to the special conditions of our planet, Earth, but a fundamental regenerative quality of all matter.

We had been blind. I had been blind. When we had supposed that life could only exist in the form that was adapted to Earth conditions, we had been as self-centered, as egotistical, as when our ancestors had supposed that the Earth was the centre of the universe and that the sun and all the stars and planets revolved around it.

But I lay awake long after that, thinking how I, a totally

alien creature, dependent on one feature of my environment, water, which was an anathema to the life of that secluded zone, could adapt myself to the circumstances I found and find a niche for myself in a strange ecology.

Even when I slept my mind must still have been battling with my problem for I dreamed that creatures from other planets had come to Earth. One required heat and could not exist in a temperature of less than that of a white-hot furnace. Another required shelter from all bacterial life whatever. A third could only live in an atmosphere of nitric acid gas. In each case they could only live if mankind were to help them and create artificial conditions for them.

When I awoke, it was daylight. I looked up at the long white slope with its slabs and steps. I stood, and turned round, and looked at my machine. Somehow *that* had to go up *there*. I had regarded the project as impossible the previous day, when I had thought that I would have to go not only up but over, and seen my time ticking out because of lack of food. Now I thought in terms of longer periods, of the years through which I might have to live on Mars.

If I lived. If I could accomplish the one essential and enlist the co-operation of an intelligence utterly alien to my own. I was desperate.

I looked over my food supply It was pitifully small by now, but I had suffered no ill effects from my strange meal of the previous day. Yet what I had must still go with me It was all the rest of the equipment on my machine that I unloaded and dumped amid a pile of rocks

I had breakfast then. Then I took a steel crowbar from my equipment and began to dig away at the first step of the crumbling rock. I chose the point with care: a place where, if all the steps were evened out in a straight road up, I would be able to drive the machine up all that slope.

It took me half an hour to even that first step out, to cut back the lip and even out and pack the debris to make a ramp below. Then I went down to my machine, climbed aboard, swung it cautiously round in a circle, and put it to the slope. I went up, cautiously but with just sufficient reserve of power, on to the slope below the second step. I stopped the machine there, and chocked the wheels and tracks.

It took me three days to make the whole ascent, camping twice on the ledges in the middle of the slope. During that time, I went twice to the crest on foot. At the crest, I moved with the caution of a hunter stalking game. I crossed the crest on my belly, and slid down to the terrace where I filled my cooking pot with the 'food' I found. Like a hunter, I was thin and grimed, covered with the powder from the rock, alert, long-haired, unkempt, and frightened. Would a creature from another planet, I wondered, show such excessive care when approaching Man on Earth? Perhaps not if he came equipped, in a vessel that made him self-contained, so that he could treat with the human race as a sovereign power. But I, aware of the chances and mischances of a planetary landing, thought I would do well to hide for a while, and watch, and study. I did not know Martians, but I did know Earth men and their reactions to anything strange and probably obnoxious.

The third night I spent upon the crest. I had brought with me, in my effort to bring everything I could, a small object-telescope from one of the sextants that had been used as navigational instruments aboard the rocket. It was through this small instrument, from a vantage point in a cleft between two rocks on the summit ridge, that I watched the valley.

During the daytime I had seen little of the creatures. There had only been the 'mother' and four or five—I was not sure which—small editions of her, basking or sleeping on the rocks. In the distance along the valley I had once imagined I could see another tribe. I had envisaged the valley as some nursery of the species, through which all the more human, animal creatures must pass on their twice-annual trek from pole to pole, and where the creatures had their birth and being before they left the valley to follow the wave of life as night-predators upon it. I had a theory, insubstantial as it was, that the creatures could not have evolved simultaneously with the Martian 'men', and that therefore they must have some other, simpler, more basic way of life, from which the continual passing of a defenceless prey had led them in a bygone age, until, following the migration, they had become masters of all the planet.

Watching from my crevice, I saw the lights in the valley bottom begin to come to life at sundown. I saw them stationary at first, as merely a ruddy glow below me. Then, after rising through the spectrum towards the blue, they began to move. One vast row, the 'mother' I presumed, glowed a steady turquoise. The others, higher in frequency, startled me with sharp flashes of pure violet. But I could make no headway with their 'language'. What I could understand was the movement, the running together of the lights, their separating and their chasing. They went round in circles like children engaged in play.

I put my glass away and watched the silent patterns below me with the naked eye. Could I rely on my feeling that the activity was play? I tried to imagine whether all life, even totally alien life, must always learn in the same way, by trial and error, by the acquiring of custom and habit which would govern all later actions. Perhaps it was not so. Perhaps some stranger kind of nervous system, unimaginable to us, could exist, something that learned its habits and way of life not as men and kittens and tigers do, by way of sport, but by some more sudden accretion of responses. But if so, the fact that what went on below me in the darkness looked like play was a hopeful sign. The difference, appalling as it was, between myself and those strange creatures, was not too great. . . .

Cautiously, careful not to step into the moonlight or to cast a shadow on the white rocks, I withdrew from my cleft.

I had seen that the creatures remained, for the most part in the valley bottom, only occasionally climbing a few terraces up the sides, but I had no wish to become the mouse for their cat-like sport, should they even by the remotest chance see my single movement. I retreated from the crest and waited for daylight, when I felt safe enough, and slept.

That evening, I took all the wire I had brought with me from the wreck. Before darkness, I prospected along the crest until I found a crack into which I could only just insert my body and yet which gave me a view of the valley and of a point on a terrace just below me. From the crack to the terrace I laid out my wire, hiding it in hollows between the rocks and burying it with rubble where it had to cross the open. On the terrace itself, I buried it two feet deep. Then I made a metal frame to protect the light bulb.

When darkness fell, I was in my crack. To my hand was the wire that led from the bulb below me back into the machine behind me and the battery By using coils and resistances in the circuit, I could cause the bulb to glow from red, through yellow, to a pure white light. I could not produce a blue light except from the torch which I kept to hand. To cover that, I had cut strips of coloured material from my clothes.

I was ready. I was prepared to make the first true and desperate contact between the human race and that which I could only suppose to be the dominant Martian species. There was no other way. Even if I had been prepared to live like a rat in a burrow in the wall of their garden home, I still lacked water. I lacked shelter. I lacked a steady source of fuel and power. Even the food, miraculously sustaining as I had found it over a short period, could not form a permanent diet for me. I needed more of everything. . .

I needed a Man Friday. I needed some one creature that knew the land and knew the ropes. I needed a Thing that I could train and use to supplement my strength, a body that could live freely in, or be independent of, that thin atmosphere and the cold. I needed an intelligence that was at home on Mars, to supplement my own.

And, above all, I needed to prove the dominance of the human species. I needed to prove to myself, as well as for all other men who were to come, that Man, even naked, with no more tools than would fit him for survival, could yet dominate an alien planet. For it seemed to me that either there was something in humanity, some grasp, some spirit, some intelligence and transcending understanding which would make all human history worth while, or there was nothing: nothing but a momentary squirming of helpless, fated life in all the myriads of individuals of our species, doomed to end and as meaningless while it lasted as cloud of bacteria that multiplied explosively in a fluid, then, having used up their food, died off and left the liquid still. Either I had in me something which fitted me to survive, even among more highly developed forms, so that Man was the chosen race that would inherit the universe as a whole, or my intelligence was a joke, a grim accident of fate, as though a worm should know its own humility, and I could not care how soon I died nor what giant's foot was raised to stamp on me and black me out.

My improvised preparations made, I was in my cleft of rock and ready for my trial. I had learned at last that even on that barren planet Mars it was not what I could do with things that mattered, but my relations with other creatures, other life, as even Crusoe had found when, after the trials and storms and shipwreck, his existence had become dependent on the savages—and the goats.

30

IT WAS IN the fifteenth year of my stay on the planet that the American ship landed in Latitude thirty-five on the southern plain, which was in summer then and which presented the same aspect as the northern flatlands when I had first seen them.

I approached the ship in daylight of its second day, walking up over the low horizon and wearing an oxygen mask and a simple cylinder. I wore Earth clothes: the last that I possessed of the overall boiler suits that we had used in our earlier though fated rocket. When I was within half a mile I could make out the stars and stripes that were painted on one small section of the vessel's side. When I was within a quarter of a mile I could see that ship lay still unopened and unmoving, as I had reason to believe she had since the instant that she landed in a beautifully timed and controlled descent.

There was a window or port-hole behind which I fancied I saw a movement, but I did not shout or wave. If they were alive, I did not doubt that they would have been keeping watch and would have seen me. I was not surprised when, after an hour of walking, and when I was within a hundred yards, a disc door began to open, swinging slowly and heavily back, and a figure in a pressure suit came out.

They had improved pressure suits since the time when I had had mine. His was of a bright metallic-thread material which did not blow up around him like a balloon. I saw him stagger as he climbed down from the open airlock port. The suit and the strange, light gravity were new to him. I guessed that this was their first attempt at moving out upon the planet. I saw him turn, look quickly at the horizon all around him, like a man not exactly afraid but like one who does not know what to expect. He bent and looked quickly at one of the scattered plants, which were in the flower stage. Then, postponing all that until later, he came on towards myself.

We stopped, face to face. I could see his head inside his helmet. His expression was one of uncertainty and amazement. I held out my hand, and I saw him look at it, but there was a pause before he brought up his own. I could sympathise with him, and might have laughed if I had been in a mood for laughing. To come to Mars and find a creature there dressed in a boiler suit, with the habit of shaking hands.

I motioned to him, towards the ship. It was useless to try to talk to him out there. I could see he was talking, for his lips were moving quickly, and his expression was of excitement, but only a faint and muffled sound reached me through his helmet. I guessed what was happening. He was giving a running description of me and of all our actions. He was using the same technique as a volunteer does when engaged in dangerous bomb-disposal: the full account of every move so that if anything happened those who were listening might know the exact move that had been wrong.

I patted him impatiently on the arm, and began to move towards the airlock. He caught up with me immediately and held me back. I felt exasperated at the delay after so many years. I evaded his grasp, which was easy enough to do, since he was clumsy in his suit, and went on towards the airlock.

The door began to swing to as I approached it. Whatever their reason, they were undecided about letting me in at all. It half closed, then stopped, then swung a little open. I began to get angry with them. I went to a port-hole that I could reach. I saw an astonished face, a head and shoulders in uniform behind it. With my finger, I wrote upon the glass, writing carefully backwards: "Let me in!"

The face disappeared, and I heard a cry and a clatter from within the ship. I turned to the airlock again, and it swung slowly open. I gave them a chance to make up their minds. The man in the space suit had caught up with me. He began to hold my arm again and talk fast into his microphone. Watching through his helmet-glass, I saw him stop suddenly, with his mouth open, with an expression of ludicrous dismay.

Suddenly he released me and motioned first tentatively, then emphatically to the airlock. Wryly, I gave him the thumbs-up sign.

There was a skeleton ladder which had descended as the door came open. I went up it. The airlock was better than ours, just as the ship was bigger. It was about five feet in diameter and three feet deep. I could stand in it with a little crouching. But my companion, the second man ever to land on the planet Mars, followed me in. We were crowded then, and though the door closed and the lights came on, nothing happened.

With the helmet six inches from my ear, and in that confined space, I could hear the man inside it talking. He seemed to be arguing fast and speaking in distress. I looked around me for any form of microphone. They must have some method of communication, beside radio, with the airlock. I saw a kind of metal grille let into the golden plastic-covered surface. Towards it, taking off my mask momentarily, I said: "What are you waiting for? Bring up the pressure!" I was astonished at the vehemence of my yell.

My companion turned, and looked at me indignantly.

There was a loudspeaker somewhere behind me. I tried to turn to see it when it startled me by speaking. It said: "Who are you? We haven't air to waste. We have to be sure you're not bringing bacterial infection in. As it is, we're going to have to disinfect the airlock."

I said: "Blast you! I'm an Earth man like yourselves, and I've lived here fifteen years. There's only one bacteria in the whole of Mars to harm you, and I don't carry that around with me!" I spoke quickly, all in one breath, and then replaced my mask. I needed to, and half my words were lost, because the air had begun to whistle in and I got a whiff of it. They were taking no chances. They had dosed it heavily with disinfectant.

We waited. My companion began to go through motions like a diver coming up to surface. He feared the bends, though he must have been breathing in half an atmosphere, and anyway the pressure change was in the wrong direction. Somebody said to him, quite clearly to my ears: "Don't be a fool, John. You'll be all right."

I took my mask off. I coughed a little in the disinfectant haze. I said: "He's disorganised. I don't blame him. So would you be if you were in this gas."

I turned round. I looked at the flush, smooth surface of the outer door. Even after all those years I could not forget the time when, in our ship, in space, it had given way. I shuddered a little, remembering that accident and all that had happened since. I wished I could feel happier then and there. Why could they not have turned up within six months of my landing on the planet? Why had it had to be fifteen years?

I felt a grip on my arm. 'John' had got his helmet off. He was a dark, thin young man with the fanatical eyes of an experimental scientist whose guinea pig is usually himself. He didn't look the type to make mistakes about whether the pressure was going up or down I guessed he was suffering from some deep emotion.

He said: "Are you British?"

"Yes."

He was quiet, looking at me. Then he said:

"You had an explorer A man called Scott. He got to the South Pole, then found that Amundsen had got there before him. Don't take it too hard if you aren't exactly popular on this ship"

I made no comment on that. It did not seem very important to me just then. They couldn't be so petty

The inner door swung open. Facing me, flanked by men in some kind of special uniform, was a U.S. Air Force General.

"Come in," he said tightly. "And congratulations."

I went in. I went forward with my hand out to him. I began to realise that it would be even harder than I thought, to break the news I had to give.

"Congratulations to you," I said. "You aren't our successors on this planet. You're the first to make a controlled descent." I looked around me. "The first," I said, "to arrive with the means of taking off again." I paused. "You're my rescuers," I added dryly. Then, more dryly and quietly still: "I hope."

31

BUT THAT was in the future. For the present, not knowing the years that were to come, not knowing if I were to live another hour, I was in the cleft upon the hill, overlooking the valley of the creatures.

They came. I saw them staring up the slope below me. I lost sight of the mother from that time forward. I had eyes only for those thin, high lights which crossed terrace after terrace towards me, up the lower slopes. They came desultorily, uncertainly, like kittens chasing a paper ball, and every now and again one of them would wander away, unseen to me in the darkness, suddenly to reappear, coming chasing back along a terrace slope.

I saw them, watched them, and felt horror at what I was doing. I was too near my light, I thought. I was too near that little winking light which attracted them.

For they were big. As they came nearer, I felt the ground beneath me quiver and I had an all but irresistible impulse to squirm out backwards, away to the outer slope. They must be big, I thought marvelling, as ten-ton yachts. And, I thought, more frightfully, what chance would a creature from another planet have of making contact with Earth children if he were no bigger than a beetle? *Perhaps* it might be more than he would have with an adult. . . .

I flashed the light in a definite sequence and almost at full brilliance. Two longs, two short, and then a pause. Three longs, and then a longer pause. And then repeat, again and again, until no creature that lived by sight could fail to recognise the rhythm. There were minutes during their ascent when I thought it was all useless, when I thought that maybe their 'mother' would call them back. But as they came, near me now, more than half-way up the slope, I saw that one, with his light organs, whatever they were, around his side and along his side, was copying the colour of my light and flashing my own sequence.

No sooner did he do so, than the others did the same. I felt faint with relief. That, I had thought, to make them watch, be curious, and try to understand, would be the hardest part.

I changed the signal. The letters in morse code, though meaningless to them, had been ZO. I was prepared to go among them by the name of ZO-zo, if only I could make them comprehend that I was an intelligent and living thing. I broke the circuit and stopped the light.

They too stopped. I could see them now, apart from their lights. They were only a third of the slope away, and in the moonlight. Each of them had halted and stood waiting. I let them wait.

One of them flashed my own signal, ZO, in my direction. It seemed to me, or it might have been my imagination, that he could concentrate his lights in a narrow beam on the exact spot where my bulb had been, some twenty yards from me. Instantly, I replied. I sent the signal back. His lights flashed on again in a blaze of colour that began at lilac and went up and out of my spectrum range.

I replied in red. He had stopped. They all stopped. They echoed my colour, like, I thought, children echoing and mocking a man's gruff voice. I switched to white again and they came charging on like terriers who see a rat.

I switched off. It may be thought madness if I say I

sensed their mood, but I was not going to have them approach me in too rash a spirit. I watched them continue to come forward and then begin to search around. Again and again I saw them call my signal. I liked that. By their own repetition of it, they would remember it, if their brains —or their responses if they had no brains—were like ours at all.

Two of them turned and went down again towards the valley like children who have tired of playing a game that leads to no conclusion. I watched them go. I had two left, who were coming on now, creeping up, I thought, on the place where my light had been. From time to time they gave my signal. I took to answering now, with one short flash each time they gave it, using minimum illumination and a dull, slow red.

The result was what I hoped. They walked rather than ran towards me, and in the moonlight, as they passed below me, I saw their shapes: like something from the bottom of our seas.

I became afraid again as I began the dangerous second stage. It was not them I was afraid of now—though I wished I had their 'mother' in my range of view—but that they would smash my bulb and my sole source of communication with them. As they went too near my light, I switched it out. I watched apprehensively as they vainly searched for it. It was only when they turned away again that I switched it on—and when one of them haphazardly came too near myself.

I invented a second signal for them. As they approached the bulb I gave the old sign, the ZO, but when they went too near, I gave three short sharp flashes and switched off. It was patience I needed then: the same sort of patience required by the would-be owner of a well-trained dog. It took me two hours to make them halt when they got that second signal, 'S', so that I knew they understood it as a negative, and during that time they twice lost interest, and could only be recalled by frantic flashing and colour changes of the light.

I lay there sweating. Two hours—three hours in all since I had first attracted them to the light—and all I had done was to teach them two words for 'come' and 'go', an affirmative and a negative. Yet, at the same time, though the needed patience was an agony, and I was stiff and weary from lying crouched among my rocks, I felt a fierce pride and exultation. It had seemed to me impossible only a day or two before that I should make any contact whatever, or invent any common language with creatures so alien to myself. The project, I had told myself, had been impossible—but the impossible I must do any and every minute now.

I had taught them to listen to me. Now I must persuade them to talk to me, to engage, in their own behalf, in inventing a language with me.

I switched off my light. When they signalled to me, ZO, I switched it on again and left it on. It was when, by chance perhaps, one of them sent 'S', that I switched it off. I saw them begin a quick exchange, a violent exchange of colour between themselves. I wished I had the facilities for a show like that. But my eyes could not follow their shades and gradations. It would be like a tone-deaf person trying to make distinctions between closely related sounds. It was better as it was.

Zo, they said, and I switched on. S, they said, and I switched off. One sent his signal clumsily and badly. I sent, in morse, the question mark. He repeated his instruction and I complied. We had gone one stage further, with another symbol.

I gave them four hours of it, and then dismissed them by sending, in reply to all their questions, the letter S, and otherwise keeping silent. I saw them lose interest and begin to wander downhill to the valley. I eased myself from the crevice and stood upon the crest.

A sharp, cold light illuminated me, with the intensity of a

searchlight. It was the 'mother', who, gigantic, was fifty yards from me upon the crest. Her light beams, emitted from two round 'eyes' upon either side of her broad, flat head, were met and focused on me. With horror, I realised I was in a trap.

Her great white beams of light were focused on me: on me, the creature that had been 'playing' with her young. Ineffectually, I was flashing my torch, trying to communicate with her as I had with her progeny, and knowing it was useless. Her lights were like a roar that turned my puny flashing into the tiniest chatter. Then her white lights flicked off abruptly and I was illuminated, instead, in a deep red glow. From her sides two ruby beams flashed out, one settling on my machine and the other searching, seeming to penetrate the very earth to my buried wire until it found it and traced it out to my light bulb, the winking light that I had used for my 'experiment'. She had the whole of me then: my machines, my batteries, my artifices, and all the power and hope I had, and she towered over me still, gigantic.

32

WHEN THE ship landed, I went to it. It was like this.

He said: "You've been here fifteen years?" He did not gesture. He was not that kind of man. He simply looked over my shoulder to the airlock, the inner disc of which was slowly closing behind me, and it was as though he indicated the Martian plain, the barren desert, the waterless surface and the arid, too-thin lifeless air.

I stood there facing him in his strange ship, accustoming myself again to the glow of electric lights on metal surfaces and to the thick, heavy, humidified Earth atmosphere that I had not tasted for so long.

There was a man in Captain's uniform standing just

behind him and on his left. Seeing that I simply stood and allowed my presence to speak for itself, he said. "How d'you get here in the first place?"

I said: "I could answer questions better if you gave me a glass of water. I haven't much time, either. I'm due to go back to where I came from in an hour."

The General called his pack off me. He gave two orders, and a group of men who had been crowded round, appearing from all parts of the ship to stare at me as I came in through the airlock, suddenly dispersed. The second order –rightly or wrongly, he gave it with decision–was that I should be given a meal or anything I wanted. Then he himself approached me, held out his hand, and suggested that I accompany him to his cabin. He was courteous and cool. Another officer asked me, with equal enthusiasm, whether I could face a plate of ham and eggs. Once I had touched the mainspring of their hospitality, it seemed that they could never do too much.

I followed the General to his cabin, looking curiously about me as I went. I did not know it then, but by taking an unproved stranger through the centre of that ship he was breaking more of his own Security laws than he or anyone else could even remember. But the situation was unprecedented, and he had to do something with me. Perhaps he thought that, since he could not interview me in the desert, it would be better to have me in his cabin than standing where we were, with a view of the engine and control rooms of his rocket.

It was like an exceedingly diminutive ship's cabin. If that were where the commander slept and lived, I could not imagine how the rest of them fared. I learned later that, like ourselves, they had fallen back heavily on submarine experience, and that many of the 'hands' were actually naval volunteers. As it was, by the time he and I were in, and two other officers had followed, as though by right, there was room only for the civilian who had come out to me only in the doorway.

"Captain Vanburg," the General said, indicating the fair-haired officer whose preoccupation was with my origin. "Lieutenant Boles, Mr. John DeLut. My name is Stilwell." Two of us had established ourselves on the berth, which I noticed was fitted with webbing to hold the occupant in in conditions of zero gravity, and the other two on the bench that faced it. Tall, dark DeLut remained standing of necessity. Somewhere behind the panelling a fan switched itself on and added its high whine to the other beating, drumming and hissing sounds which spoke of a rocket-ship maintaining its atmosphere and temperature and pressure in an alien environment.

"Gordon Holder," I said. "Engineer of an unofficial British expedition that left Woomera fifteen years ago. The expedition was not successful. I am the only survivor."

They digested that. Looking at their faces, I could not tell if they had heard that our expedition had gone off or not.

It was DeLut who burst through our reserve. "One thing seems clear," he said excitedly. "Mars isn't all like these deserts we've been surveying!" Having said it, he had to move away from the doorway, for a steward entered, bringing me the meal I had accepted.

I looked at the ham and eggs and wondered if my digestion would cope. There was a cup of coffee as well as a glass of water on the tray and I could hardly take my eyes off that. I did so momentarily to look at DeLut over the steward's shoulder. "If you mean there's some place on Mars that can produce food like this, you're wrong," I said.

Vanburg said sharply: "You haven't starved."

The General waited until the steward had gone out again. Then he said: "What's this about going back to the place you came from in an hour?" He had the authority. He made it clear that his were the questions to be answered first.

I told them in my own way while I ate. I was surprised at my reaction to the food. When I first saw it, my appetite went into rhapsodies about it. When I began to eat, it was different. It seemed to me that the taste was not quite as I remembered it. My teeth were in a poor state too, and I was not used to chewing. It seemed I had not remembered the power and patience required to masticate a slice of ham. Before I was half through it, my jaw was aching and I gave up. The egg I managed, and the cup of coffee was like a smoker's first cigarette after a long, long time.

I told them about our take-off, our accident, and how I had crazily decided to try to land on Mars. It seemed to me that I should tell them, to begin with, something that their own experience would enable them to understand.

"It was just luck that the ship cracked when she landed," I told them. "If she hadn't, I'd have been like yourselves, thinking of the possible bacterial infection of different kinds of life. I would have had to make experiments until I was convinced that even the inert part of the Martian atmosphere was breathable without ill effects. By the time I had decided, by trial, to bring my pressure down, and begun to look for a source of oxygen, I would have been too late. My own air supply would have been exhausted. As it was, I was plunged right into it. I either lived or died. I lived, and after that all the machines I built, or rather altered, from the wreck, grew only from my immediate needs. I succeeded in distilling Martian air because that was the only way I could hope to produce oxygen quickly enough to be of any use to me, and because anyway I had already been moving in that direction when I compressed and decompressed it to precipitate out the water. I was just lucky. I did those things quickly that I had to do quickly if I was going to go on living. The really troublesome thing, the problem of finding some sort of food that would sustain human life indefinitely, I never did solve really. Oh, I found things that were edible. That is a different matter.

Dr. Bombard did that twenty years ago, when he crossed our own water desert, the Atlantic, on a rubber raft, though he ruined his digestion in the process."

I paused at that. They were following me closely I could see. Lieutenant Boles had discovered his function in the gathering. He had taken a notebook out and was taking notes. But they were all grimly holding back their unasked questions and were willing to keep silent only so long as I continued.

"I could have done the same for a while," I said. "I had begun to make certain brews. These plants you see out here. At a certain time of the year they produce a fruit. By breaking that down with earth bacteria, I succeeded in making a kind of mess of yeast. And there were other things. Certain sugar-carbohydrate substances produce themselves here by a peculiar process in a kind of mineral form. But there is no doubt about it. If it hadn't been for my present hosts I would have succumbed to some deficiency disease or other, either scurvy or beriberi or something of that sort, some ten or twelve or even fifteen years ago."

I saw them tense. They knew that they had reached the crux of the matter now.

"You can see," I said, "that I owe them a kind of gratitude. One in particular. He won't be really understandable to you. He isn't quite to me, after fifteen years. But it's him I represent. It's his point of view that I've come to put to you."

33

FIFTEEN YEARS earlier, I had not expected to survive.

It was from behind that the interruption came. I was conscious of a new blaze of light, cutting into the ruby beams, from that direction. Involuntarily, I turned. It was one of the youngsters that I had last seen disappearing down the valley. Seeing the lights above, he had evidently returned. Could I attribute human emotions to him? Could I say that he was intrigued and puzzled? Certainly his lights were deployed in the same way as were the gigantic red ones. He with his white lights was searching me and my equipment and my machine with all the absorption of a child who had just discovered that a kitten lived.

I heard a sound behind me. It was the mother moving forward and I turned in time to see her bearing down. To attempt to run from her was as hopeless as it would have been to run from an earthquake. I had an instant of pure terror as I saw her bulk above me, and then the lights around me changed to green.

It is hopeless to attempt to convey the beauty of that colour. I could call it winsome, or pleading, or rueful with a touch of laughter, but there simply has not been on Earth such a colloquy of light. We are born of a race that has lived, for long ages, as far as its emotions are concerned, by ear and sound. We are affected directly by exhortations, and cries, and screams of agony. Even our lower creatures, born of the same ancestral forms, communicate briefly with danger cries and warnings, with love and mating calls, and the others of their species respond to their emotions. To us, the sublime is almost always sound, and there is nothing in our knowledge, nothing but the echo of playing elephants in a symphony, which can match the communications those Martian creatures make with light.

The green came from the smaller creature, and the mother stopped. Blue-green it was, the childish pleading, and it was answered by a slate-grey-green, that even to me in my terror conveyed a 'no'. But they were not steady those lights, at that stage. They came and went and wavered, and seemed to explore the resources of an area of the spectrum. To my eyes, wide and fearful, it seemed that the lights that played above my head were cut and mixed: as though my eyes, for all their staring, could not comprehend, no more than alien ears can understand the finer inflections of our speech. I deduced a 'please', a 'no' as one does on hearing a foreign language to the vocabulary of which, and even the grammar, one has not a clue. And, to me, it seemed that the mother became uncertain in her emotions. From time to time she flashed a glimpse of red again, and then whole moments of her lightning 'speech' would be suffused with red, so that it was red-green, red-blue and red-yellow that she 'spoke', only, a moment later, to be changed to an ethereal violet which ran to blue and green without the red.

I, on my knees between them, felt for my hidden wire, my switch, my key. I switched on my lamp. I sent the signal for 'yes' and then the question mark. 'Yes?' I said again, and again 'yes?' and 'yes?' It was the only way I knew to plead. Oblivious then, and blind with terror, I crawled to my machine. I took up my water can, and opened it, and again sent 'yes?' I let a little oxygen leak out from my tank into the air, and again sent 'yes?' It was the only way I knew to plead, to demonstrate my needs and my weakness to them, desperately, in some mad hope that they would think of me as a creature that needed help, not something to be killed.

As soon as I had become active, they had become 'silent'. They stood, on either side of me, in a kind of radiance of their own creating. Only occasionally, as I demonstrated this and that, and sent my eternal plea of 'yes?' would some communication pass above my head from the younger to the elder.

I stopped, exhausted. I knew no more that I could do. And the mother moved away from me, down into the valley.

I followed, or tried to follow, with the young one close beside me. When I came to a place I could not descend, he paused and waited, then went ahead and smoothed a path for me, clearing and levelling the ground so that I could descend. I followed him, and limped thus into their camp on the valley floor. Oxygen was something they could not understand, but, as dawn broke quietly as a first radiance among the peaks, he led me to a cavern in the far hillside, and there, as he left me and I entered all alone, I heard a murmur and tinkle. There, deep in the hillside, and flowing by I knew not what subterranean channels from the polar regions was that which was as incalculable and rare on Mars as a hot stream or a flow of naked lava would be on Earth: a tiny runnel of water which found its way through a cavity in the limestone and fell perpetually in the darkness into a cavern, a shaft, of unknown depth.

He knew: that was what overwhelmed me. He, the young one, had understood my hopeless, desperate signals. I lay in the darkness, taking off my mask and burying my head in that heaven-sent pool, drinking and drinking as I had never drunk in my life before, then putting on my mask again and gasping with exhaustion, oblivious of a rumbling in the mouth of the cave behind me.

It was some time, and broad daylight before I staggered back to the entrance of the cave, to see my machine which had been placed there, to discover how and if it were damaged, and to start, or hope to start, my oxygen-making plant. Only, as I approached it, I saw a shadow across the entrance.

He had built a wall, a vertical wall, to keep me in. He had penned me like a sheep in a fold, like a white mouse in a cage. It was only then, looking up at a triangle of sky above that high white wall, that I realised that I was as far as ever from gaining control of even a young one of the Martian species.

Far from making him my Man Friday in that desert world, it was *he* who was keeping *me* as a kind of pet, and it would be I who, if I wished to raise my status, would have to display my value to him.

34

THE TENSION had increased in the cabin of the rocket. The four of them were all looking at me: DeLut standing in the doorway, Lieutenant Boles on the bunk beside me with his notebook in his hand, Captain Vanburg, big and fair, frowning in the effort to understand, and the General whose face had become a mask.

"You mean," DeLut said, a gleam of excitement entering his dark eyes, "–you mean–I'm the biologist here–you mean there are intelligent creatures on this planet?"

Looking him in the eyes, I answered: "Yes."

"What kind—" he said. "Dammit, you know the sensation this will be on Earth! What size are they? What shape? What sort of civilisation have they? And where do they have their towns and villages? How do they live in–*this?*" He waved his hand to indicate not the scene inside the rocket but the desert that lay outside it, the endless plain with which they had just become acquainted, the dearth of life, the low temperatures and the thin cold air.

I told them. I confined myself to a physical description. To my surprise, they accepted the size. They must have been prepared for that. But my description of appearance, of physiological detail, and of things which lived in comfort inside their hides, independently of atmosphere or cold or animal needs, except for food, seemed to daze them and raise a doubt. I could see it in their eyes.

"And you say they are," DeLut said again uncertainly, "intelligent?"

Once more I answered with emphasis: "Yes."

"He asked you," Vanburg said, his heavy face lined with caution, "what sort of social organisation do they have?"

"A complicated one," I answered. "Based on a family system."

That got him no farther. He wanted something he could grasp and hold on to. He said: "What do they make and do?"

I told them: "Nothing."

They sat there and stared at me.

"They hunt," I said. "They eat. They sleep. They die."

Captain Vanburg's face had a frown that I assumed was patience. After a silence, he said: "You've been with them fifteen years. It's not for us to say they haven't what you say they have."

I faced them steadily. "All right," I said. "Have it your own way. They don't build houses. They don't make machines. They don't go to work at eight o'clock each morning and knock off at five o'clock at night. And they don't build rockets and fly between the planets. So they are not intelligent."

The General said: "Captain Vanburg didn't deny your statement, Holder."

"They have a language," I said. "They talk with light waves as we do with sound waves. Only they don't express themselves in words. They don't have a written language with precise meanings. If you see them talk, it's as though you saw a symphony in colour. But maybe that isn't an evidence of intelligence either. You might say that our birds communicate with one another with sounds. Some people say glorious sounds. Yet they say a bird has no intelligence."

They were all still looking at me: puzzled, stubborn, patient. Boles suddenly remembered his notebook and wrote something in it. I imagined him writing: "Communicate with lights like birds with sounds." I gave them time, and then I told them.

"They have had intelligence enough for this," I said. "When they realised that I couldn't produce colour-patterned light waves, they learned a code I taught them, based on the morse code. They learned it quickly and easily, but took no further interest in it except as a means to talk to me. And they realise the meaning of your arrival here. They knew I was the first, and you are the second, and that soon there will be more and more men coming to their planet. And to them it's as though they were threatened with a plague of troublesome ants."

They looked, for a moment, troubled. They could not conceive of the minds of the creatures I was telling them about. They could only imagine them as being like themselves or like some other Earth creature. They wanted to ask questions, but they did not know what questions it was right to ask.

"Or worse," I said.

They knew then. I saw Vanburg's lips tense. The General's eyes took on the hard, cold look of a man expecting war.

"It was my fault," I told them quietly. "Before I knew them perfectly, before I'd thought out all the possibilities of what might happen in the future, I had told them too much about ourselves. They had asked me, indifferently, not very interested in my answer, if there were any creatures like themselves on Earth: things, they intimated, of the same size and tonnage and importance. And I, like a fool, told them that there were. I mentioned whales, creatures that were able to reach their size on Earth despite our heavier gravity because they spent their whole lives suspended in a fluid. You understand. I was trying to impress them with the similarities between our planets. I was trying to convince them of the kinship of all life."

"You needed to do that?" the General said. He was wondering what armaments these creatures might possess.

I did not answer him. In the cabin of his ship, which I hoped would take me back to Earth, I told him only what I had to tell.

"They said: so those, the whales, were the dominant species on our Earth. I said they weren't. They wanted to know about the intelligence of whales. I said we did not know. All we did know was that they had brains of greater size and complexity than man's. Then they must be dominant, they intimated. And I was a fool. I was intent on impressing them with my own importance. I told them no, on the contrary, it was we who hunted whales. We were not interested in their brains. We boiled them down for oil."

They thought about that and understood. I had almost forgotten how good and quick and practical the human intelligence was.

"So," the General said, "you've told them that we won't harm them? You've told them that we aren't in a position, and won't be for a hundred years, to dispute their planet with them? And you want to go back now, and tell them that we come in peace?"

I could see why he had been chosen for his mission. He had all the practical determination and opportunism that made a leader. He came from, and was the latest of, a long line of pioneers. He might have been Cook telling the Aborigines who then owned all Australia that the white man did not come to harm them. He might have been one of the first Americans telling the Indians that all the settlers wanted was a few square yards on which to live. He might have been an armoured Conquistador promising the first Aztec he met the peace of God, or an Englishman promising mutual co-operation to the Polynesian islanders. And, like all those forerunners of himself, he believed that what he said was true, as indeed it was for him, and for the moment only: for a man who's job it was to deal with a practical situation on the spot.

"That," I said, "is the general idea. Only there is one slight difficulty. They have had me with them for fifteen years. And they have got fixed ideas about us and about our science. For instance, they are under the impression that even you, the first expedition to land and take off again, would like to take a miniature specimen of themselves with you, a young one, say. And they think, rightly or wrongly, that at the first opportunity you get, you will dissect one. Then you will discover what they imagine to be a fact: that they have substances within them which would be of infinite value to the human race. They are, I've told you, more highly developed forms of life than we are. What we would find in them might be of more value than any vitamins or ambergris or fish-oil. So they envisage that shortly men would come back to Mars, and set up a factory, and ride out in killer tractors to drag back their bodies. And all, you understand, in the name of medicine and human love and pity—which it would be, they see quite clearly, as long as mankind thinks only of himself and his own needs."

They looked affronted.

"You forget," I told them, "that when you see them, these creatures will be no more than gross animals to you, just as you are tiny animals to them. They don't have houses or a civilisation as we know it any more than we have a civilisation as they know it. Your only contact can be through me, and that is tenuous—a groping in a gulf of darkness. They themselves aren't certain how much of my intelligence is natural and how much is due to the time they have spent on training me to understand them. And if I bring one of them to you, and translate your remarks and questions to him, and translate his answers, it'll look to you like a circus trick. You'll have no more cause to believe in his intelligence than you would in that of a performing horse."

I gave them a moment.

"Which is why," I said, "they ask for tolerance. I have to go back now—my hour is up and I have only come to you on parole. Their suggestion is this: that you change one of your men for me, and leave him as an ambassador or a hostage. He can be a scientist. He can study them. And you can exchange him when you wish. They will permit a landing of one ship a year. In that way, we can live in peace. They do want peace."

They stared at me. Slowly, Vanburg said: "And you will go back to them, on those terms?"

I thought of a creature that I knew as Eii. He had been the first. It had been he who put me in the cave. I nodded.

The General said: "Suppose I agreed to this arrangement. How could I guarantee that other nations would keep it? The Russians are treading on our heels. Their ship may arrive here any day. Your own countrymen will be the next. They aren't going to accept our statement that we have exclusive rights for one ship a year. And if they break the agreement, what happens to our hostage?"

I looked down at the cabin floor.

"They don't know about that," I said. "I didn't tell them about our competing nations I never mentioned our habit of making wars. I was not a fool They think of us as a kind of termite as it is. And it's our misfortune to be shaped like the creatures that are their source of food. One word of that will convince them that we belong to a totally lower order. That we should kill not only other species but also one another will be as repugnant to them as the cannibalism of the savages was to Crusoe on his island."

When I looked up, I saw that they did not understand The idea that I had been a kind of Crusoe would have been comprehensible to them. But that *I* had been Man Friday, that I, with all my technical accomplishment and engineering had been proud to work up even to that relationship with an alien race. . . . It was impossible for them to grasp They were men of action and they judged by doing. Were they not, proudly, the first to fly in the gulfs between the stars and planets?

35

IT WAS a light in darkness, a single flickering illumination in the shadow that lay across the entrance to the cave. It was Eii, named such because that was my translation of the initial flickering of his light before he learned to signal clearly.

There was no wall across the cave-mouth then. None was needed since I had learned to live permanently within the cave for my own protection. There was only the water, and the food they gave me, and the equipment that Eii had brought once, incomprehensibly to me, from the distant wreck. I had thought then that he understood my needs. I had imagined for a moment that he knew how necessary fuel was to me and parts and spares for my machines, metal plates with which to build an airtight room. But he did not. He had brought it as stuff, as pertaining to my nature.

They had not helped me to make the neon tube I was using to reply to the flashing signal. They did not help me in my laborious daily work of mashing the fruit they gave me, fermenting it, and distilling off an alcohol for fuel. That I even needed the blue-white crystals that they used was a surprise to them. I had had to win them round slowly to an understanding of my needs, night after night flashing and elaborating the code from its crude beginnings.

Even when I had all I needed the 'conversations' went on. Eii had exemplary patience. Perhaps he was one of those rare children that can really keep a pet and train it.

"You were not here?" he was flashing now, his carefully dimmed light-organ still illuminating, in ghostly fashion, the limestone walls. And I, sitting in the chair I had made, with the neon light mounted above my head upon a stand, and a morse-key on my knee, understood his meaning. It was all, in the early days, like that. It demanded a mental leap, an understanding of what it was for which we had no word. I had to explore, above all, how his mind worked, and he had to guess at mine.

"I was not born here," I said. I saw his light dim as he memorised the new signal, the word 'born', which he would read not as letters, as in morse, but as a single comprehensive whole of twelve dots and dashes, and remember perfectly, but perhaps not quite comprehend

"You have said another world."

"At a distance far from here."

He dimmed again, and then his light changed colour:

"There are no such distances as you have tried to say."

"Distance," I said. "Not time. Distance is the one that is reversible."

Startlingly, in bright yellow light, his answer came: "To you it may be like that." Then he shifted his bulk and went away, leaving the cave-mouth empty.

The next night he was back again. It was always during the period of darkness which was his 'day'. He drew in across the entrance to the cave like a train into a station. Even before he was fully in position, his light was flashing at me so that I had to read it as I turned.

"How did you cross this distance?"

I hastened to reply to that, running to my chair. The rarity was that he should ask 'how?' at all Even then I suspected that it was not really what he meant It was only a minor variation from his eternal 'why?'

"I crossed distance by constructions such as you have seen me make here. They are useful these constructions. They could be of use to you"

"'Use?'" he flashed. "Why 'use'?" He baffled me. It seemed I would never have done with the alien quality of his mind and be able to explain myself

"They could do things for you," I said.

"It is strange," he said, "that you who spend all your time in doing still admire constructions which do your doing for you."

That was the first time I came across an attitude to doing which was all but incomprehensible to me at the time and which later proved almost impossible to convey to the Americans in their rocket.

"I cannot breathe or eat or live in this world unless I have equipment," I told him for the thousandth time.

"You would do well to die I think," he said. "You and those you say are like you."

I became furious. I touched the rheostat on my equipment and stepped up my battery voltage. "Our deficiencies are our strength!" I said. "Because we have needed covering and all the warmth and comfort you possess by nature, we have had to invent our ways and means. We have learned so much that now it is possible for us to cross those distances we spoke about. Everything would be possible to you too if you would take an interest in construction. At least let me assist you. Let me make constructions which would be of use to you!"

He thought about that. When he thought, his light dimmed but went neither on nor off.

"Everything possible?" he said. "By way of doing?"

"To do is to learn!"

He flashed a negative.

"To know how is to know why!"

He flashed a negative.

I lost my temper completely. "You know nothing," I told him. "You do not know of what things are composed. You do not know the distances between the stars!"

His light came on with the green of laughter. "It is you who know nothing, I assure you!"

Another night he appeared and lay as a black mass across the cave-mouth and said nothing.

"I have something for you here," I said. "I have watched you in this valley for six months now. I have seen how you are dependent, those of you who stay here, on the twice-annual trek of the living things who must come through.

You kill and eat and then for six months you starve. But I will build fences into which you can drive your prey, and then you will have them always, when you need them."

He was silent, with the utter disinterest of indifference. It was only that his light came on, with a pale blue light, like an eye that sleepily opened.

After a while, he said: "It is a pity that you cannot be what you are, instead of trying to be more or different."

I tried to understand him. Desperately I tried to understand. For fifteen years my life was dependent on it.

I said: "Our lives are short. We do what we can with them while we have them."

There was a long pause then. When he flashed again it was with a concept that was strange to me. Perhaps I did not understand it. He said: "If you were to stop doing your life would be as all eternity. Why do you strive? What do you strive towards?"

I stared at him, at the darkness where he was. I tried to understand but could not. I became indignant. It seemed to me that he was decrying the value of all effort. I did not stop to think why a denial of the use of doing should so affront me.

"We strive to know all things and to do all things. We think of the future of our race and how we will expand and deploy ourselves among the stars and fill all the spaces of the universe with ourselves!"

He was silent—lightless—for a while. Then he answered gently:

"I think you strive only to gain the strength and comfort that your bodies lack. I think there are too many of you already. I think that each of you feels weak and does not know why or what he is nor where he leads. You crave for power, because power means safety. You crave for strength because you are weak and uncertain of yourselves. You crave for knowledge because you know nothing. You crave to conquer the universe because it is so vast and you are so small. You think always that if you can know a little more, if you can travel a little farther, you will stumble on some secret which will transform your nature. But your nature is what it is. It is that you should try to change."

He arose and went away. In the darkness, I was left wondering about what he said. Not, of course, that I wondered whether all our doing was not of use to us. It must be. A hundred million human brains could not be wrong. But I wondered for the first time and with despair whether anything I could do for more perfect beings, who did not need to strive, could be of any use to them. I began to sense, in his alien nature, a totally different set of values: an appreciation of the nature of things which left me cold and fearful since it was a denial that I and all I stood for had meaning or could be of any kind of use to him.

When he came back, it seemed that he, and not I, had solved my problem. He came to the mouth of the cave and obscured the stars, and his light winked brightly, cool and blue.

He said: "In your own world, not here, what are the things you do?"

I thought. I was more cautious now in my replies. I seemed to be living from moment to moment in an inner anguish.

"We make shelters," I said, "and covering for our bodies. We strive to make the climate of our world, which would be cruel to our nakedness, more suited to us. We make heat and light and warmth. We prepare our food until it is delicious to our senses. We train our offspring so that they will inherit the skills and knowledge that we have. And, beyond that, we strive to see our world and learn what we can of all there is to see."

His cool blue light said gently: "If you were to succeed in these things?"

I looked into the darkness that was the shadow of his outward shape, and did not reply. How could I tell him that it was not success we hoped or even strived for—how could I admit that our stage of development was such that each generation must laboriously repeat the actions of its fathers and add so little, so very little to them? That every man born must face the same problems, and, though he might be more skilful in his efforts, could never hand on a completed task? It would be too easy for him to say, I thought, that our hopes were vain no matter what they were or could be, and that, before one man could travel beyond the stars, a million million other men might die.

He said, softly it seemed, such was the quality of the light: "Suppose that some day you are entirely successful in your doing. You have active groups of men, you told me, who strive always for efficiency. Suppose their efficiency becomes quite perfect, so that like us you no longer need to do or strive, but may live without effort solely at a touch of a button on one of your constructions. Suppose, since you are creative, you can create what you will, with no greater effort, and travel freely, and acquire all knowledge. What will you *do* then? Have you some more perfect construction in your mind? Or do you envisage only means and not the ends? Is it simply the power to do which you lack and therefore are so jealous of, or have you a purpose in mind, which you will achieve, when you attain perfection?"

I did not reach for the key which was in my lap, I did something that I could not conceive of myself as doing. I, a man bloodied by fate but undefeated, burst into tears. It was as though, for the first time in my life, in any life, it seemed to me that my striving was not only useless but no longer needed. I—it was an hallucination, it must have been—saw a picture of myself in that state of beatitude that he painted for me. And I knew that that, the state, was what I had craved and wanted. I had never, neither I nor any man, considered what I would do with it. I had never found it possible to populate Heaven with actual people.

His light, his seeing, not his speaking light, played over

me. He saw my distress in the cave that he had given me. He must have sensed my physical and mental wretchedness.

He said, so gently and softly, and with a violet radiance: "If you could conceive of the end to which you would use all power, if you had it, you might find it unnecessary to have the power. The end and purpose of your existence might be accomplished by simpler means than all the complexity and trivial life-consuming action that you tell me of. Why should I waste your time, which is shorter even than our own, in building fences for us which, for millenia, we have done without? And why, for that matter, should you strive always to make things, to achieve things for yourself?"

I snatched at my key. With my left hand, I slammed at the switch which made my neon tube glow red. I heard my high-voltage generator hum as I turned my communication system to maximum power.

"Why do you torture me?" I said. "Why do you take away from me the little that I have? Am I not sufficiently wretched in this cave? I tell you that my race has its sole strength in doing. We are the ones who can accomplish. We are those who will penetrate your world and all the universe. It is true we do not know how we come to live, or why! It is true that ultimate purpose, and a knowledge of the meaning of all things are just what we lack most! But do not taunt me with it! Such talk is dangerous. When we have conquered your world, and found out what and how it is, *then* we will know more of the answer to your question 'why'. Or at least we hope we will. That is our faith. We have the faith that we will find a meaning. We will find a meaning not only for our own lives, such men of us as are living then, but we will find a meaning for the lives of all the men who have lived and died before us. We! We whose weakness, whose need for action, has been turned to strength! Then, then by knowledge and conquest, we will find our final purpose!"

He answered me with a golden glow, with words he spelled out slowly:

"But if I were to tell you your final purpose now, and avoid that effort?"

I did not answer. His seeing beam played on me again and saw me sitting rigid in my chair. Around me the limestone sparkled with his sudden brightness.

He said: "This code of yours is not adequate for the purpose. But you have begun to use the colours. You must watch and try to understand. You must widen those dim eyes of yours. You must cast aside your preconceptions."

I looked. I had no alternative but to look. I saw him slowly come into illumination all about his form. I saw a transcendent multiplicity of colour that slowly began to change. And he was young! I had that one and only shocking thought. He was but a child among these creatures, like a boy who had conversations with his pet and tried to teach it human hopes and human speech! I stared at his blue and gold and green and red, and, as he had told me, my eyes widened at his changes, at his pulses and transfiguration. I sensed, rather than thought in words, the concept that began to form.

I cried out. I covered my eyes with both my hands. I fell down before him on my knees. I cried out, aloud, in words: "No more! Enough!" I bent my head. I would have buried it in the sand. It seemed to me, suddenly, that a ghastly blackness took hold of me. I screamed, and screamed again, then knew no more.

When I came to, I was lying in my cave in daylight. My machines were softly humming. The oxygen was pouring from my mask as though someone—it must have been Eii, though I never saw him touch any mechanical contrivance before or since as though he understood it—had turned it on to full.

I looked around me wildly. I staggered to my bed and

slept. I slept one night, two days, and Eii did not come back to me until the succeeding night.

His lights were sombre then, like a boy's face in remorse when he looks at a puppy he has injured. Hesitantly in the darkness, he flashed the dots that were his name, then mine.

I stirred, and he saw me stir, but I did not reply.

He said: "I am sorry that I misled you. I have spoken to others. We would be glad if you made a fence for us. Could you do that when you feel well again?"

I looked at him, unspeaking and unthinking.

He said: "Let me persuade you that we really need it. You know how helpless we are at doing things. We would benefit greatly from practical assistance in our world."

I believed him. I had to, to live at all. I did my best to believe him for fifteen years of life-in-death when the sanity of human companionship, its sense of mutual support and certainty, was denied to me. I worked steadily in and about the valley, and the question of ultimate human purpose was never raised again. It was only that when one of the Martian creatures came up to me, I would try to avoid him and go away. Even with Eii, I was glad that he did not try to talk to me as he had been doing, but merely praised me, fed me, and found practical work for me to do.

It was like that, I doing work and Eii providing me with materials that I needed, until, by means of an instrument I had constructed on the cliff above my cave, I was able to tell Eii one day, seeking him out for the purpose since he had somewhat lost interest in me, that other men were coming. I had seen the ship circling the planet after detecting it at a range of a hundred thousand miles. In my telescope it had the aspect of a small silver cigar-shaped lozenge among the stars.

I cannot even now say why I told him instead of simply setting out to meet the men and escape with them. I am utterly certain that Eii would not have stopped me.

36

WE HAD moved out of the cabin into the centre of the ship again. We were paused hesitantly before the airlock on the metal gallery which formed a platform when the ship was horizontal, a ladder when it was in space. There were still the same four around me: the General, DeLut, Vanburg, and Lieutenant Boles, but other men, of junior rank, found occasion to pass closely by us, and pause, and stand around, in the course of their duties in the ship.

The General said crisply: "I can only suggest that you don't go back. We've seen quite clearly that their conditions are incapable of fulfilment."

"We can't give hostages," Vanburg said. "It isn't the American way. Apart from which, we can't guarantee a situation that we can't control."

I looked at the airlock. Already it was wearing off, the feeling that my rightful place was far outside it. My place was there, with men, in a hot, humid atmosphere that reeked of machines and oil. In a world of practical action, incisive speech, and decisions made firmly despite all risks. That was the way men lived. I had come near to forgetting it. All the same, I had to go.

"I'll tell them what you say," I said. "I don't suppose you can even commit yourselves, the Americans, to one ship a year? I'll tell them, of course, that you won't molest them."

"Our intentions are entirely peaceful," said Boles sincerely.

"Tell them that we'll put it to our Government," the General said. "We are only the navigators. We are under orders. As to how much you tell them about what the possibilities really are, I leave that to you. Personally, I would say that if the Russians get a ship up here there's going to be an almighty scramble for this planet. No one's going to rest until it's been prospected thoroughly for radioactive ore."

I looked at the airlock door again. It was a great, circular sheet of metal, and a member of the crew was already standing by the screw-type handles. I only had to nod and he would open it and I would go inside. The pressure would go down, and I would be sure to feel it, that quite desperate sense of nausea and deflation which I realised I had been living under and enduring all those years. Then I would go out on to the Martian desert. Perhaps for the last time. Perhaps in an hour or two I would be back.

Or perhaps not. I had, already, met the American ship. I might be used, similarly, to meet the Russians when they turned up. It might be an utterly endless process. I stood there wondering just how much I really owed to Eii and his fellow-creatures. For years, though I had helped them, they had lived in apparent oblivion of me.

DeLut said: "Just before you go, Holder." He frowned at me as I turned to him.

"Just this," he said. "Supposing these creatures are all you say they are--intelligent, cultured, and all the rest. The fact remains that they are deficient on the practical action side. This sort of thing has happened before you know. The Indians were highly civilised when your first East India Company Merchants went out there. You British found it necessary to take over the administration of that country. It didn't mean that Indian culture did not have its advantages and its value. Just that it didn't stand up to our sort of civilisation."

"Well?" I said. It seemed to me that he was putting the situation mildly.

"Only that I seem to remember that there were hostages there from time to time. My history of the British Empire isn't what it might be. But I fancy that most of them got slaughtered."

Vanburg laughed grimly. "We might put it even more clearly than that to Holder: that it didn't make any difference in the end. The fact that the British had the technical know-how to get out there made it inevitable that they would win as soon as any bother started."

"You might tell them that," the General said. "I gather that they are under the impression that they are our superiors. But it isn't ethics or philosophy; it's skill that wins. You could put that to them mildly and suggest that it would be wise if they gave a safe conduct to yourself."

I nodded and thanked them. Clearly, they did not understand. Ants might talk like that, if they were prospecting taking over the human world. What efficiency of ours could compare with theirs? Ants would, to the ant-mind, win. But it only looked as though the situation was like that on Mars. They had not had the advantage of talking to Eii in the cave.

I took a step to the airlock and watched the crewman begin to turn the handle. "Though in this case," DeLut said, "they don't seem to have any ostensible civilisation anyway. They're merely hunters who eat raw meat. Typical aborigines. You're wasting your time on them."

It took all the strength of will I had to step into that airlock. I think they all knew, those who stood around, that they would only have had to make a show of physical restraint to make me succumb willingly to their blandishments. But that was not their business. They had to make contact with whatever there was on Mars, and my presence, unexpected as it might be, was a way of making that contact as smooth as possible. That I was willing to risk my neck in the effort was their good fortune.

I went in, and the door clashed to behind me. The inner light came on as it did so, and I heard the screws made fast. A pump began to rumble somewhere. I waited as the pressure went slowly, so slowly down. I should have done the bending exercises that DeLut had been hazed into doing when coming in, but I was too busy thinking how fateful events in my life seemed to be tied up with going into or out of airlocks.

It was as bad as I had expected, the physical sense of cold and weakness. I had forgotten so quickly what it was like to live with vitality reduced at a too-low pressure. Then the outer door swung open and I stood looking out at the yellow desert with its ground-clinging blotches of crude plants.

I thought then of changing my mind. It was the depressive effect of the pressure and the desolation. I knew that, cave or no cave, I could not endure another fifteen years of that. Yet what could I do? Advise Eii other than that his best chance was to keep me, let me do the talking to all these people? With one hostage at the beginning, and assuming that the situation was carefully handled . . .

Heavily and wearily I climbed down the ladder, turning my face towards it as I descended. From a port-hole in the ship they were waving to me. I did not reply. I put them from my mind: they and their heated air and food and companionship and certainty. Too well I knew their feelings. It is something basic in our nature that makes us take actual pleasure in a struggle with the unknown side by side with other men. They, I was sure, would even be prepared to die in style. But I walked out across the stony ground alone, clumsily and slowly as I did on Mars.

After I had gone a hundred yards, I could still feel their eyes boring into my back, wondering if they would get a glimpse of what would come to meet me. They would have a long wait, I thought, as I struggled out, away from them, across the surface. And nothing at the end of it, for I had two miles to go and then I would cross a rise of ground and be lost to view.

I walked head down, watching the ground, careful not to stumble over stones or plants. For a while I did not know what was happening to me. I had seen a rocky ledge some hundred yards ahead and I thought I ought to be about up to it by then.

I raised my head and it was still a hundred yards ahead, though the plants and stones were disappearing beneath my feet. A green plant and a flat stone shaped like the outline of a cat were just a yard ahead. They disappeared beneath my feet.

A green plant and a flat stone shaped like a cat. They were ahead again. . . .

I stopped, I looked back. I was walking in the right direction. The silver rocket-ship was just behind me. Just behind me and not twenty yards away. . . .

The airlock burst open. DeLut came out. He was waving wildly. I guessed he must be shouting. Behind him came two more men, carrying something that looked like a folded stretcher. There was no one else around. They must have intended the stretcher for myself. Yet I did not believe that I had been stumbling in my tracks.

I stopped and waited for them to come to me. I watched them walk. They walked all right. They put one foot before the other. But it was as though they were swimming against a current. They made progress and got precisely nowhere. The two men with the stretcher were wearing clear-type helmets and I could see their faces. Their expressions were those of consternation and astonishment. They looked around them wildly. They well knew that they should have been up to me by then.

I walked back to them. I made progress quite well in that direction. It was only when I turned and looked away again and at the horizon that I seemed to detect a bend in the fluid air. It was as though the level land was corrugated slightly, or as though I were looking across a hot surface on a summer's day on Earth, and seeing the light refracted in waves of heat. A mirage maybe. . . .

It was all round the ship, and deep, that bend or twist in air and earth. It was like a fluid into which one penetrated just so far before one realised what was happening. Only some people, I noticed, could penetrate farther than others before they reached a standstill, while the other side of the bend was like the ground-line on a graph of a declining curve: the farther one got, the nearer one came to it but the less progress forward could be made.

I put my helmet close to DeLut's. I saw his startled eyes. I yelled: "In infinite time one could get across. This is just the sort of trick they would play!"

He yelled back: "For God's sake come inside! That's an order. You're to come inside the ship again at once!"

I grinned at him and shrugged my shoulders. I wondered if Eii had known that I would come back to him empty-handed, or if he had guessed that I would, or if he had merely wished to see if I would try to come back at all. I hoped it was the latter. I hoped that he was feeling as pleased that I had tried to come back to him as I was because I did not have to go.

He had certainly solved the problem of an ant-invasion. Without, I imagined, really doing any thinking. Practical matters were, after all, so far as he was concerned, a waste of time. He ate, he slept, he thought.

37

DAY AFTER DAY on the journey back it went on. The ship seemed to lie motionlessly among the stars, and we, inside her, floating in zero gravity, climbed around the galleries and hand-rails and met each morning in the General's cabin or the control-room.

Usually there were just the four of them at each interrogation, all of them specialists in their way, even the General, who might have been said to be a specialist in effectiveness. Certainly he had been chosen for that, as one of the younger, top-flight men who could be given charge of a rocket expedition to another planet as a rare opportunity, such as came to few in peace-time, to make a name for himself and build up his career. But now he did not know if his expedition had been a success or an utter failure. The view that would be taken of it, by the press and in the Pentagon, would depend so absolutely on my testimony. Either he had been outwitted by creatures which would be thought of as no more important than savage beasts—as though, in an earlier age, he had discovered Africa but been frightened away by elephants—or he had made the first human contact with a quite new plane of reality, a quite new form of knowledge.

It was not to be wondered at that during those days and weeks and months he and his little group of officers sought to possess themselves of all my knowledge, to have an answer for everything ready when the time came, to be prepared to answer any criticism as to what they could or should have done.

At first it was the simple, incontrovertible, unbreakable, appalling fact of what had happened that most concerned them. They brought their mathematician into the room three mornings running, and confronted him with me, both of us talking different languages, in an effort to elucidate in the slightest what had happened. They charged him, even in my presence, with the task of framing some coherent explanation, some scientific hypothesis, which was at least sufficiently related to what was known to attract the interest if not the conviction of other scientific minds and to be embodied, however implausibly, in an official statement.

"Captain Vanburg has got to write a report," the General said. "I've got to initial it. And I've got personally to report—for God's sake, man! Suppose they call me to the White House. What do I tell the President? Do you think I can give him this sort of stuff?" He tapped a paper that lay on the table between us all. A paper containing a single line of figures which Jaeger, the thin, pale-eyed mathematician, had put forward as one conceivable explanation.

"I don't see what else you can tell him," Jaeger said. "What is there to say, except what happened and the mathematical hypothesis for it? What d'you expect me to do, put all post-Einstein thinking about the universe, and something far beyond it, into simple words?" He looked trapped and scared. It was his business to explain what he was talking about, and he could not. He did not happen to be Einstein. He was just an operator of abstruse formulae that worked in practice for calculating the progress of a rocket from A to B.

"Holder!" the General said. "You know those creatures! You know what they think. At least you know what they think *about*. You talk to him. You try to explain what you know and let him try to explain to you what it means in theory *supposing* it has some sense to it. Between you—for God's sake, you've got two months!—you build up something cut and dried!"

"Well, I look at it this way," I said. "Eii—that's the one I told you about—he'd kept me too long to want to injure me. He sent me to you probably wondering if I'd revert to type, as he maybe thought it. He probably wondered if neither I nor anyone else would go back to him. Perhaps he thought we'd try to declare war on them or something. But he also probably thought that the system of hostages, if it worked, would be a way of keeping us in check. What he saw, in effect, was that I was loyal to him but that no one else was coming back with me, as he would have expected if there was to be an exchange. So he thought quickly. Or maybe he didn't even need to think at all. How am I to know? He knew our limitations all right, and he simply used them. He treated us as a nuisance that should not be allowed to spread around his planet."

They listened to me. Vanburg and the General, when I first began speaking, looked at me with a kind of hope. What people or things did was obviously within their sphere of interest, as was why they did them. But in the end they suddenly began to look more lost and concerned than ever.

"How?" the General said. "How, how, how? Dammit, Holder, don't you see that that's the question we have to answer. To say this creature did it—that doesn't mean anything! Except that maybe he'll do it again and again, each time we land, and that we'll get no farther! For God's sake talk to Jaeger and tell him how!"

I thought about that. I was accustomed to Earth air and pressure again by then. I felt comfortable and relaxed, and I was going home.

"So far as I can tell," I said, "he does it not by asking how at all, but by asking why."

That broke up that meeting. Or rather is was a quite hysterical giggle from Boles that broke it up.

In the afternoons, I used to sit on my bunk and write this journal. I had to think how I was going to live when I got back to Earth. I decided that to write my story, and have it ready to sell to a publisher and to newspapers for serialisation would be a good beginning. In fact I decided that it should put quite a nice little nest egg in my bank.

Another morning they tried a different tack with me. The General was not there when I went into the cabin. He was busy, Vanburg said. "But," he said, looking me in the eye, "I've got to get to the bottom of this. Those are my orders."

"Fine," I said. "Where do you want to begin? With what I said to Eii and what he said to me, or with my early wandering in the desert and how I first saw the creatures? Probably all we have to do is to decide which bit is going to be most helpful."

He did not seem to look at it that way. For an instant he looked baffled. Then he said: "Let's concentrate on what they actually did to all of us. You know them. You explain it."

"I can't," I said. "That's Jaeger's job. He's the mathematician."

"For Jesus Christ's sake!" Vanburg yelled at me. "Haven't we been through that before? He can't explain it! If you can't tell us how, at least tell us *what* they did! Use your own words! Tell it like you'll tell it to a reporter when we get back! Tell it like we weren't there, that we'd no idea of it, and let's hear what you say!"

I wondered what the General had said to put the fear of God into a Service Captain. But they were my rescuers. I didn't want to harm them.

"If you think it's going to help, I'll do my best," I said. "If I had to tell it to anyone who didn't know, I'd put it this way. I don't think this creature I called Eii loved us. I myself was hardly worth bothering about to him, one way or the other. If he'd had any difficulty doing what he did, he'd have been more ruthless. I don't think he'd have had any difficulty fixing us so that we couldn't take off again, but then he'd have had us on his hands. And he didn't actually want to kill me. He might have done that easily when he first saw me, but you know how it is with something you've had around for quite some time. So he just wanted to fix us so that we couldn't walk around and be a nuisance. He probably remembered the confusion he and I used to get into when we tried to talk about space and time. He probably realised as well as I did that he and I saw the universe in quite different ways. I saw plane surfaces and solids, but for all I knew he saw atoms and electrons or whorls in space. He was different, that's the thing you've got to understand. Different and lazy and always ready for a short cut when it came to action. Unless it was hunting or feeding or such things as even lazy humans sometimes do for sport. You shouldn't think of him as a creature without instincts, only as one with far fewer than we have ourselves. So, knowing our limitations, he built a kind of fence around us. I never told you what happened about the fences I tried to build for him, did I?"

Vanburg looked utterly hopeless and in despair. DeLut said: "No you didn't. Go on. This is interesting. This may throw some light on things."

"I went to a great deal of trouble about it," I told him. "You know how I told that when I first saw the creatures shaped like men, I tried to fence them off my plot of ground. I used all the wire I could, but I didn't use a high enough charge to be effective. Well, in the valley there, the sort of household settlement of those bigger creatures, where they must have been born, like the crystal plants there, from a different kind of evolution from our own, they relied on the six-monthly passage of the wave of life. Once every six months all living mobile things on Mars came pouring through. For creatures of their size, who could wait six months between meals, that was convenient. All they had to do was have a big twice-annual slaughter. But the wave of life crossed their valley on a wide front. What I wanted to do was wire off the majority of the little passes, use a sufficient charge this time, and absolve them of the necessity even to stalk and hunt."

DeLut's dark eyes had a look of fanatical intelligence. He said: "Go on!"

"I did what I could," I said. "Eii indicated that he had no objection if I wanted to do something on the lines that I suggested. So I did it, working in the daylight of course, and in the sunlight. I spent six months on it. Six Martian months, which is twice as long as that would be at home. And then I found that it was all useless."

"Useless?" Vanburg said. Despite himself, he seemed to show a momentary flash of interest.

"The things never went near my fences anyway," I said. "Naturally, when the wave of life came through, I went to see it. I felt annoyed when I saw that Eii and his fellows had pulled certain of my fences down and seemed to be using some of the lines I had closed as those on which they chose to lie in wait. They didn't even bother to conceal themselves either, which looked desperately inefficient to me, who had climbed a hillside and was looking down on them from above. But the men-like things came on, and then, for the first time, I felt my own kinship to them, and felt pity for them. Because, by some process I couldn't understand, they seemed to walk deliberately, and without reason, right into the traps that had been laid for them. It was—well, it was a slaughter. It wasn't nice. No nicer than what goes on in our slaughter-houses, though we hide them from view, and we could, if we wished, live on a vegetable diet exclusively. These creatures like Eii couldn't. They were only doing what they had to do to live at all."

DeLut said quickly, before Vanburg could interrupt again: "Why d'you think those creatures, the prey, followed the lines that were chosen for them?"

I thought about that. "I don't know," I said. "Maybe there weren't any other lines. I saw one or two start off sideways, but they did not seem to get anywhere, and they soon came back. Perhaps you're right. Perhaps they ran up against the same sort of time and space shift that we did. But if you look at it that way, you'll have to accept another thing. That this barrier, whatever it is, that they put up, isn't a new or an invented thing. It's just a natural part of life to things like Eii. Like—well, like spatial concepts are to human beings, though there is no indication that ants ever looked up and wondered what lay in the sky above them. There's no indication that they have even wondered about, or realised there was a sky or 'up' at all."

Vanburg felt he had got somewhere in that first session he had conducted without the General. He hammered away at it for a fortnight, asking me questions and getting DeLut to ask them, but he never got any farther. As the General put it, when he came in on the sessions again: "You've established another reason for thinking that these creatures can do whatever it is they did. But you didn't need to establish that. They did it. We were there."

"At least," DeLut told him, "we have Holder to take back to prove that we have been there. Otherwise we haven't much else in that line, except some photographs and some stones and moss."

The General looked at him sourly. He did not approve of DeLut. Too intelligent, and too ready, far too ready, to shoot off his mouth.

I worked steadily on my journal and it slowly became accepted throughout the ship that they had been to Mars, landed, discovered an Earth man there, and then, when they tried to walk out across the plain, got nowhere. Kept going, but made no progress. And all they were going to be able to do about it, when they got back to Earth, was to tell their story and stick to it.

After two months, when we were still in space but nearing Earth, the General said: "I'm going to put in a positive recommendation. The next ship that goes has to have a big reserve of power and fuel endurance. She'll land, and if she comes up against a barrier, she'll go out into space again and come down again wherever it was they were trying to get to. If necessary, we'll explore the planet that way, in hops and jumps. It'll take time. It'll take a devil of a time and a mint of money. But we'll do it in the end."

DeLut looked at me, and I looked at DeLut. We both said nothing.

That evening we went, as we had got into the habit of doing, into the little two-man navigational astrodome that was built in near the tail. There was no navigation going on there then, and there had not been for a week or more. The sun and Earth were large on the bow, though invisible to us, and the navigators were all working where they could get sights.

It was dark with the night of space in the astrodome, and

cold. Far, far away, where we could only just pick it out among the million stars, the red planet swung.

We both stood there, looking at that tiny orb, for a good long time.

"Do you think," DeLut said, "that the General and people like him will ever succeed in annoying them too much? Do you think that people like us will ever convince them of the need for action and that it isn't sufficient for them to go on, just living and dying, as they are?"

I knew DeLut by then. I looked below the surface of his words.

"You think it would be better?" I said. "Our action and their—what shall we call it?—sensibility? I doubt if in a million years we'll understand one another well enough to unify our outlooks."

"I'm a biologist," he said.

I waited until he was ready to speak. I was in no hurry. I was content to look through that jet-black sky, with its brilliant lights, to the little planet which I had never thought to leave again.

"They have no competition," he said. "That is why they are what they are. If there was competition, they'd feel the need for action. But without competition, by Earth laws, they must degenerate. They must have degenerated. They can only be a shadow of what they were."

He too was in no hurry. The spectacle of space was not one that either of us were likely to live long enough to see again. And, unlike the General, he gave me time to think about my answer.

"By Earth laws, you said." I thought some more. "Maybe that was our mistake," I said.

"You mean to imagine that the same laws would apply? But science is science. What is true in one place is usually just as true in quite another."

I wondered. I said: "In the social sciences?"

He said: "I'm trying to think about it. Suppose we ceased to have wars among ourselves. Suppose we really got on top of our environment and wiped out all diseases and even made the roads safe to walk and drive upon. Suppose we had all, every one of us, all the power we needed and all the goods and comfort and convenience. At the moment, that is what we strive for. It is the goal of our sciences and our economics and our politics. And yet, biologically speaking, the achievement of that goal would be fatal to us. By Earth laws, we would degenerate. In ten generations we would be a race of morons. But they, Eii and his fellows—they seem to have begun, been born into that situation which is at once the sum of all our hopes and the crux of all our fears. If we could only learn from them, if we *could* make contact, more contact than you have made in fifteen years—that is if they have not degenerated. If they have found some other occupation that is not doing, fighting, striving. . . ."

I moved my body in the astrodome so that I seemed to look 'down' on Mars. It was for the last time. Soon we would be within the pull of Earth's gravity and all our thoughts and hopes would be towards what lay ahead. Mars would be a rarely seen speck on the sky, directly overhead and obscured by cloud and smoke.

"I don't think so," I said.

He was silent. He waited for the meaning of my statement.

"I don't think we'll have the patience," I said. "We won't make contact. People like the General will treat it as a practical problem. They will see it that they have been opposed by power on Mars, and they will seek to overcome it with greater power. I would even go so far as this. In the end, I think we'll win. We'll conquer the strange beasts of Mars just as we conquered the strange beasts of the continents and the oceans. And, in conquering, we'll learn nothing from them. We'll not even treat them as creatures who could see or feel or know. We'll kill them and use them, as I told you, for their bones or blood or oil. Perhaps rightly so. Eii and his kind have no sympathy to spare for their own Martian creatures who are shaped like men. But we will do it, and we will go on. After Mars, it will be Venus, Jupiter, Saturn, Mercury, and the rest. Then other solar systems in our galaxy, then other galaxies and out beyond space itself. I think we will be, at last, a movement of life transcending time and space. I doubted it at times, on Mars, but now I think it. Only it will only be sometimes, in quiet corners, out of the main stream, in places where hope is no longer possible and when action has become futile and been seen to be futile for generations at a time. . . ."

We looked down on Mars and became conscious that she was receding from us. The ship was tilting. Already, unknown to us, the moment had come and the decision been taken to turn the vessel over, rockets down to Earth.

"Then?" DeLut said. "In backwaters, in places where conditions are like those on Mars, where competition does not exist, and the spirit can live in a material desert sufficient only to the body's needs?"

"Then," I said. I watched the stars begin to move and turn. They were moving, the whole brilliant universe of them, past the windows of the dome and seemingly against the outer darkness. "Then," I said, "the other thing will be born. That knowledge that is of being, not of doing. Those inferences which are of actualities, not events. Those permanencies which come of a losing of the sense of time: when a moment is eternity, and eternity is a moment, and all ages are embodied in an instant. Perhaps then, for some of us, sometime, the work of our active lives, which consists of no more than moving matter around in space, will be seen to be the futility that it is, and our preconceptions about structure and dimensions will disappear . . . leaving something else."

Mars, as we watched her, disappeared. Instead, expected,

yet unexpected in its blinding glare, came a transfixing ray of sunlight and the gigantic flaming orb swung up into our heavens.

"Then," DeLut said, "all knowledge we have now will be in a crucible, in a state of disintegration and re-forming, like atoms in that furnace."

We stood there, pale white figures scorching momentarily beneath a dome of glass, and then retreated.

www.ingramcontent.com/pod-product-compliance
Lightning Source LLC
LaVergne TN
LVHW090943080826
845145LV00003B/877

* 9 7 8 1 9 4 7 9 6 4 7 2 3 *